Queen in the Making

30 Week Bible Study for Teen Girls

Queen in the Making

30 Week Bible Study for Teen Girls

By

Reverend Onedia N. Gage, Ph. D.

Other Books by
Reverend Onedia N. Gage, Ph. D.

Are You Ready for 9th Grade . . . Again? A Family's Guide to Success

As We Grow Together Daily Devotional for Expectant Couples

As We Grow Together Prayer Journal for Expectant Couples

As We Grow Together Bible Study: Her Workbook

As We Grow Together Bible Study: His Workbook

The Best 40 Days of My Life: A Journey of Spiritual Renewal

The Blue Print: Poetry for the Soul

From Fat to Fit in 90 Days: A Fitness Journal

From Two to One: The Notebook for the Christian Couple

Hannah's Voice: Powerful Lessons in Prayer

Her Story: Bible Study

Her Story: The Devotional

Her Story: The Legacy Journal

Her Story: Prayers and Journal

ILY! A Mother Daughter Relationship Workbook

In Her Own Words: Notebook for the Christian Woman

In Purple Ink: Poetry for the Spirit

Intensive Couples Retreat: Her Workbook

Intensive Couples Retreat: His Workbook

Living A Whole Life: Sermons Which Provide, Prompt, and Promote Life

Love Letters to God from a Teenage Girl

The Measure of a Woman: The Details of Her Soul

The Notebook: For Me, About Me, By Me

The Notebook for the Christian Teen

On This Journey Daily Devotional for Young People

On This Journey Prayer Journal for Young People

On This Journey Prayer Journal for Young People, Vol. 2

One Day More Than We Deserve Prayer Journal for the Growing Christian

Promises, Promises: A Christian Novel

Six Months of Solitude: The Sanctity of Singleness Notebook

Tools for These Times: Timely Sermons for Uncertain Times

With An Anointed Voice: The Power of Prayer

Yielded and Submitted: A Woman's Journey for a Life Dedicated to God

Yielded and Submitted: A Woman's Journey for a Life Dedicated to God An Intimate Study

Yielded and Submitted: A Woman's Journey for a Life Dedicated to God Prayers and Journal

Library of Congress

Queen in the Making:

30 Week Bible Study for Teen Girls

Purple Ink, Inc. Press

For Information:
Purple Ink, Inc.
P O Box 300113
Houston, TX 77230

www.purpleink.net ♦ www.onediagage.com

onediagage@purpleink.net ♦ onediagage@onediagage.com

ISBN:

978-1-939119-60-5

Printed in United States

Dedication

To My Queen in the Making, Hillary!

To the Queens in the Making who I serve

Actively and passively,

Up close and from a distance.

To the Mothers and Fathers of those

Queens in the Making

Thank you for letting me impact her life!

God's Words

Deuteronomy 6:5 (NIV)

[5] Love the LORD your God with all your heart and with all your soul and with all your strength.

Psalm 139:14 (NIV)

[14] I praise You because I am fearfully and wonderfully made;
  Your works are wonderful,
  I know that full well.

Jeremiah 1:5 (NIV)

[5] "Before I formed you in the womb I knew you,
  before you were born I set you apart;
  I appointed you as a prophet to the nations."

Dear God,

Thank You for making me a girl! Thank You for Your provisions for me and Your other daughters. For You to love us the way that You do is amazing! Thank You for validating us and giving us work to do. Thank You for calling us Your daughters.

Thank You for Your compassion, leadership, plans, forgiveness, and wisdom. Lord, I want You to be proud of me and I hope that I don't disappoint You as much as I previously had. Help me to overcome temptation. Help me to hear from You and discern Your voice. Help me to be obedient to Your urgings and Your will.

Thank You for Jesus and the Holy Spirit. I need an intercessor and You have sent one to me. Thank You for creating me. Thank You for the plans that You have for my life.

Thank You for helping us girls to survive a world that does not really embrace us the way You created us. They make it difficult to be a girl. Help us to continue to be faithful. Create in us a clean heart. Help us to keep the faith which we need to have a great relationship with You.

Thank You for empowering us to be powerful and wonderful. Thank You for making us fearfully and wonderfully.

Thank You for this book and these girls it will serve. Thank You for using me to complete Your work.

I pray for these blessings in Jesus' name.

Amen

Dear Queen in the Making,

God loves you! I love you! In this world in a short period of time, you have seen a lot of information. Some of what you have seen may not have been great. Some of what we have seen is awesome.

In this study, I want to insure that you know that you will love yourself more as a result of growing closer to God. Be prepared to release your fears, forgive those who have harmed you, intentionally or unintentionally, and understand that you have a purpose.

Seek to be enlightened by what God will reveal during this study. This study may initially cause you to examine and explore parts of yourself that you did not consider important or lovable. Experience love through God's word in an outstanding way that you have never had before.

Consider forgiveness of yourself and others so that you can have the peace of God describes and provides for each of us: for you.

Immerse yourself in this study so that you can experience the fullness of God's promises. You will need this information at some point in your journey as a girl. This may seem unnecessary; however what we do know is that the devil is after everything and everyone who belongs to God. That means you!

As I consider the differences between your childhood and mine, the biggest difference is the technology that you have. While on the one hand, the technology and the internet is a good thing with all of the information, there is a HUGE downfall because you are exposed and overexposed to the world in an unfiltered way. Your eyes have seen and your ears have heard some 'filthy' things that we cannot undo with a backspace button or the delete key.

With that in mind, we as leaders, mentors, parents, and teachers are praying for your healthy survival of this overexposure, especially those things that we will never know that you have ever seen or experienced.

May God Bless You!

In God's Service,

Rev. Onedia N. Gage

Dear Parents:

I pray your strength in the Lord through these lessons. I have had some of the most enlightening experiences by teaching young ladies about God, life and her future.

I have only an inkling of what your journey has been like. I actually have no idea of what your journey has been like, however, I do know that your journey is not new and it is not the first or last time a parent will have that same experience.

Take refuge in God in this season. Keep in mind that God is in complete control! God also knows your circumstances and your situations. God has not forgotten you and your tears and your prayers.

God is clear about what you stand in need of. God also hears your prayers and knows the desires of your heart.

Help her through this 30 week study. She needs your prayers, support, and guidance. Feel free to submit your prayer requests to me via phone, text, email or by mail.

Likewise, I am convinced that as parents, we need each other. I also authorize you to actively act those older parents did before us where we did not have any privacy: go through her phone, read the messages, view the pictures, check the internet browsing history, know her passwords, keep tabs on her friends, ask questions of her about the details of her daily life, require her to come home at a curfew, teach her the manners she needs to survive in this world, require her to have standards for the life you dream of for her and remember you are the parent and consequently have the last word. And by all means, take the bedroom door off of its hinges if you cannot get the door open or if you cannot get her out of her room.

You have exactly 6,574 days to turn her into a queen from your little girl. Use this time wisely. These days seem like a long time but if you are not careful, they will pass you by. Keep in mind that you are first in line as her source for information, the person who can influence her, and the orchestrator of her spiritual foundation. This time requires your full attention.

Be a bold, courageous parent!

She needs you to be bold and courageous in order for her to be a Queen!

Just trying to parent a Queen in the Making too,

Reverend Onedia N. Gage

Dear Facilitator/Ministry Leader:

For every girl we meet in church or at camp or at school or wherever, that girl needs us to be the intercessor, the leader, the adult, the guidance, the sounding board, the listening ear, and the advice giver. She does not need, nor should she expect us to be her friend.

This study is designed to help her navigate the toughest areas of her life. She looks up to you: she watches you. You mentor her—initially without your knowledge. You influence her without your knowledge or consent. You change her mind and sometimes her heart, and certainly her behavior all because she has been in your presence.

Study. Pray. Fast. Meditate. She depends on your attention to God. She needs your total dependency on God.

Show her what you know. Share with her your story so that she may understand that what she is experiencing is not new and is survivable. Remind her that God does not make any mistakes and she is a plan for which God has a purpose.

Engage her at a HIGH level! She needs a level voice to counteract the voice of the internet and her friends who also gather their information from the biased internet. She needs affirmation and reminders of her purpose and His calling on her life.

Be careful! What you teach, you will be held accountable for as well. You will have to espouse and embrace these lessons. You will be convicted in the areas where you have avoided God.

She needs your help. She needs your love. She needs your protection. She needs your patience. She needs your forgiveness. She needs your permission to forgive herself. She needs your full and undivided attention. She does not know how to ask for your attention, but she desperately needs it.

I am praying for you. You will need to fast and pray regularly on her behalf.

Thank you for serving her and not avoiding her.

In God's Service,

Reverend Onedia N. Gage

Table of Contents

THE NERVE TO DREAM

By Onedia N. Gage

You have the nerve to dream
And expect others to do the same
The audacity

You know dreams don't come true
You know that we don't leave our circumstances
You know that we cannot convince others to believe falsely

You have the nerve and the audacity
To expect us to dream
When there is blight and slums and
Economic hardships

You still dream for better than we have it
Better than <u>all</u> our ancestors
We have more educated
We have more educators
We have more leaders
We have more politicians
We have more wealthy
We have more
. . . yet you still dream of more

You dream that still more can happen
The audacity of you
And the nerve
And the gall of
You to tell our children that they
Can have more than we have
Define more
How much more

More with what?
Less?

Dreams.
You still do it
And in the worst of times
By perception
By the naked eye
But up close they deserve every opportunity to dream
They deserve hopes
They deserve dreams
They deserve the audacity to look at me and
<u>Know</u> that they too can have what we have
And have more of it.

You still dream.

Reprinted from **In Purple Ink: Poetry for the Spirit**

Queen In The Making

30 Week Bible Study for Teen Girls

WEEK ONE

Who is God?

Who does He say that you are?

Genesis 1:1-31

Genesis 1 (NIV)
The Beginning
[1] In the beginning God created the heavens and the earth. [2] Now the earth was formless and empty, darkness was over the surface of the deep, and the Spirit of God was hovering over the waters.
[3] And God said, "Let there be light," and there was light. [4] God saw that the light was good, and he separated the light from the darkness. [5] God called the light "day," and the darkness he called "night." And there was evening, and there was morning—the first day.
[6] And God said, "Let there be a vault between the waters to separate water from water." [7] So God made the vault and separated the water under the vault from the water above it. And it was so. [8] God called the vault "sky." And there was evening, and there was morning—the second day.
[9] And God said, "Let the water under the sky be gathered to one place, and let dry ground appear." And it was so. [10] God called the dry ground "land," and the gathered waters he called "seas." And God saw that it was good.
[11] Then God said, "Let the land produce vegetation: seed-bearing plants and trees on the land that bear fruit with seed in it, according to their various kinds." And it was so. [12] The land produced vegetation: plants bearing seed according to their kinds and trees bearing fruit with seed in it according to their kinds. And God saw that it was good. [13] And there was evening, and there was morning—the third day.
[14] And God said, "Let there be lights in the vault of the sky to separate the day from the night, and let them serve as signs to mark sacred times, and days and years, [15] and let them be lights in the vault of the sky to give light on the earth." And it was so. [16] God made two great lights—the greater light to govern the day and the lesser light to govern the night. He also made the stars. [17] God set them in the vault of the sky to give light on the earth, [18] to govern the day and the night, and to separate light from darkness. And God saw that it was good. [19] And there was evening, and there was morning—the fourth day.
[20] And God said, "Let the water teem with living creatures, and let birds fly above the earth across the vault of the sky." [21] So God created the great creatures of the sea and every living thing with which the water teems and that moves about in it, according to their kinds, and every winged bird according to its kind. And God saw that it was good. [22] God blessed them and said, "Be fruitful and increase in number and fill the water in the seas, and let the birds increase on the earth." [23] And there was evening, and there was morning—the fifth day.

[24] And God said, "Let the land produce living creatures according to their kinds: the livestock, the creatures that move along the ground, and the wild animals, each according to its kind." And it was so. [25] God made the wild animals according to their kinds, the livestock according to their kinds, and all the creatures that move along the ground according to their kinds. And God saw that it was good.
[26] Then God said, "Let us make mankind in our image, in our likeness, so that they may rule over the fish in the sea and the birds in the sky, over the livestock and all the wild animals, and over all the creatures that move along the ground."
[27] So God created mankind in his own image,
in the image of God he created them;
male and female he created them.
[28] God blessed them and said to them, "Be fruitful and increase in number; fill the earth and subdue it. Rule over the fish in the sea and the birds in the sky and over every living creature that moves on the ground."
[29] Then God said, "I give you every seed-bearing plant on the face of the whole earth and every tree that has fruit with seed in it. They will be yours for food. [30] And to all the beasts of the earth and all the birds in the sky and all the creatures that move along the ground—everything that has the breath of life in it—I give every green plant for food." And it was so.
[31] God saw all that he had made, and it was very good. And there was evening, and there was morning—the sixth day.

God is THE Creator! Of all things! God is our Creator. God started from scratch—a clean sheet of paper—God created the world from nothing. Absolutely nothing. He Created the Earth, all of its contents, all of its animals. Then He created us. He created light and darkness.

He created us: Each of us! God created us in His image. When we define His image, the words which come to mind are Creator, creative, detailed, organized, kind, loving, forgiving, and powerful. He created us to possess those characteristics as well.

God made us to exhibit those characteristics at all times to everyone.

God made you to achieve His goals and His goals alone. Because God created you, that means the plans that He has for you (Jeremiah 29:11) will materialize. This is hard for most of us. We really cannot imagine what those plans are or how they will come together, but God knows.

Since God created you and used Himself as the example, we are defined by God's definitions and His criteria. This means that the outside world cannot define you. We need to remember that when someone tells us something negative about ourselves, we need to REJECT those negative thoughts and words. Rejection means do not internalize, do not consider what was said, and do not embody the characteristics that they are trying to cast upon you.

God made you in an excellent manner. You are fearfully and wonderfully made (Psalm 139:14).

You create the image others have of you through your behavior. If you are unhappy about what people think and say about you then change your behavior.

God says that you are His child. He loves you. He loves you more than you love yourself and the sum of your love and that of others for you as well. God created you for His service and His glory. God created you for great things that He designed for you.

God created you without fear and without judgement of others. God created you to love with Him and His spirit.

You will hear great things about yourself and you will hear terrible things about yourself. You have to filter the negative away from yourself. So when you consider who you are and who you think you are and who others think you are, measure it against what God says. When it does not agree with God, REJECT IT! Even when and especially if it is your family and others who are supposed to love you does that. REJECT IT!

God expects you to be love, forgiveness, honorable, long suffering, loving, joy, peace, kind, good, faith, gentle, and have self-control. Galatians 5:22-23.

God says that you are all of that because He made you so.

God provides us with the Holy Spirit so that we can remain closely aligned with God.

Don't let anyone who say that you are someone that God says you are not.

WEEK ONE REFLECTION

1. What do you know about God? Who first told you about God?

2. What do you think God thinks of you? What do you think of yourself? What do others think of you? Why does that matter?

3. How does someone else's opinion of you cause you to change how you feel about yourself? Why do they have that much influence over your opinion of yourself?

4. How do you think that your character and image, details of your mind and your heart, and most importantly, your soul were designed?

____

____

____

5. What does it take to upgrade your image of yourself, and consequently, your image in the presence of others?

____

____

____

6. Why does your image matter? Who do you really represent: yourself, your parents/family, God? What behavior exhibits the best representation of who you really represent?

____

____

____

7. What do you need to change so that you are properly representing the God who loves you and who keeps you?

____

____

____

8. When you look at yourself in the mirror, do you look at yourself with criticism or disdain? Try to look at the image that God sees. What do you see?

____

____

____

____

WEEK ONE PROJECT

1. **Design a mirror, personalized with your favorite things, colors, and activities.**

Look into the mirror every day. During that time you cannot criticize yourself or scrutinize the details of your face or your hair or your body.

2. **Design a poster for the scripture: Genesis 1:26-27.**

[26] Then God said, "Let us make mankind in our image, in our likeness, so that they may rule over the fish in the sea and the birds in the sky, over the livestock and all the wild animals, and over all the creatures that move along the ground."
[27] So God created mankind in His own image, in the image of God He created them; male and female He created them.

WEEK ONE JOURNAL

WEEK TWO

God Loves You Extravagantly

[16] For God so loved the world that he gave his one and only Son, that whoever believes in him shall not perish but have eternal life.

John 3:16 (NIV)

[13] But for right now, until that completeness, we have three things to do to lead us toward that consummation: Trust steadily in God, hope unswervingly, love extravagantly. And the best of the three is love.

1 Corinthians 13:13 (MSG)

God loves you! God loves you beyond measure. God sent His son to save us because of His love for us.

Imagine if your parent(s) were told when you were conceived that you will save the world, but in order to save the world, you must die and suffer. What would your parent(s) do? Would they have been willing to do that despite the outcome? God did that for us through Mary and her husband, Joseph.

Your parent(s) would not be willing to do that. I would be still asking why do I have to give up my child to save an ungrateful world, including my ungrateful self.

But God loves us! He did it. Mary complied. How else does that love become your everyday life?

God loves you daily. God loves you through your storm and your rain and your good times. God's love comes out when you need something and someone shows up unexpectedly and provides your needs.

God's love shows up in people who are genuinely concerned about you.

God's love shows up when you get that job that you need to provide for your family. God's love shows up when your diagnosis started out terrible but returns with a healthy future.

God loves you because He created you. In His image. In His likeness.

Nobody will ever do more for you than God will so be clear that when He demonstrates His love for you, His love is everlasting—through every storm, every rainbow, every sunshine, every tear, every smile, and every triumph.

Love is a verb! God does it every day! God demonstrates His love for you when He wakes you up and when He feeds you and when He clothes you and when you survive illnesses and when you overcome adversity and when you get favor that you obviously don't deserve.

Favor is defined as being granted an unmerited blessing, especially if you did not expect that blessing. Blessings are blessings because they are unexpected and undeserved.

God's love overrides the world's intentions and the tragic outcomes.

God's loves causes you to survive and to overcome. Then God tells us to love extravagantly: God, yourself and others, especially those who do not love us. Loving extravagantly means loving people who are not deserving of your love. Loving extravagantly means loving yourself when you actually hate yourself, just because God loves you and told you to do so.

God loves you infinitely and through infinity. In Ephesians 3:17-18, Paul tells us that God loves us with a width and length and a height and a depth that completely covers us and provides us with power.

Love covers a multitude of sins. Love completes us. God loves you before anyone and God loves when everyone else quits. God loves because everyone quit.

Free yourself to love, to receive love and to be love. God's love can be duplicated and replicated and can be internalized and externalized. The best thing is that God's love does not cost us anything.

Lastly, love extravagantly also means that you are not on a budget—you can love without regulations or limitations or discrimination. You are not going to run out of love. God is your replenisher. Your love will not run out so stop keeping it to yourself. When you keep it to yourself, you don't even love yourself more. So what good is it to keep unused love to yourself? There are people who are assigned to love you and there are people when you are assigned to love.

Love.

Love.

Love.

WEEK TWO REFLECTION

1. Define love. God's definition. Your definition. The world's definition. What's the major difference between those definitions?

____

____

____

____

2. What does it take to love others? Is it difficult? Why? What happened?

____

____

____

____

3. Why are you rejecting love?

____

____

____

____

4. Do you feel unlovable? Why or why not?

____

____

____

____

5. Who loves you? Why do they love you? How do you know?

____

____

____

6. What do you do to love others? How do they know that you love them?

____

____

____

7. Does love cost or is it free? Is it real love if it costs something? Explain.

____

____

____

8. Do you love certain people differently than others? Who? Why?

____

____

____

____

9. How do you feel when you know that you are loved? Unconditional love?

____

____

____

10. Do you think you need permission to love yourself? Why? Do you need permission to love someone else? Why?

____

____

____

____

WEEK TWO PROJECT

1.   Write a love letter to God.

2. Write a love letter to yourself.

3.   Write a love letter to your parent/guardian.

4.   Write a love letter to a friend.

WEEK TWO JOURNAL

WEEK THREE

God created you on purpose, with a purpose,

To be a purpose

"Before I formed you in the womb I knew you,
  before you were born I set you apart;
  I appointed you as a prophet to the nations."

Jeremiah 1:5

[11] For I know the plans I have for you," declares the LORD, "plans to prosper you and not to harm you, plans to give you hope and a future.

Jeremiah 29:11

"I set you apart," says the Lord. Not says your mother or your teacher, but the Lord. They are just repeating what they heard.

The Lord formed you in your mother's womb. God selected your parents, formed you between them, and started your legacy. You ARE NOT anyone's mistake! God created you on purpose. God created you to do His will—a specific job, designed just for you. Accept God's word as truth: God created you, knowing exactly what He wanted you to do.

When God mapped out the time of your conception, the time of your birth, and the circumstances of your existence, God also knew your job. He made Jeremiah a prophet. Maybe God gave you influence over your family and friends. Maybe God gave you the ability to see the good in others. Maybe God gave you the ability to help people heal. Maybe God gave you the gift of teaching. He possibly gave you the gift of prayer. All of His gifts requires you to be alive to impact the audience God designed especially for you and the message He equipped you with. God blesses you because you are His. You belong to God.

When God created you, He had plans for you—plans you may not know or understand or even see right now. Some of the plans that God has for you does not evolve for years. Remember Jesus lived 33 years before some of those plans materialized. Some of God's plans take longer than others. David was appointed at age 12 to be king but David did not serve as king until several years later. God was preparing David during this time for the time he would serve.

You are being prepared for your work as well.

God does not create us to hurt us. God created us to work with Him and to serve Him and to glorify Him. Your work brings Him glory.

Start believing in God.

Stop believing the negativity that others want to infuse in your life. Do not listen to those who say that you are worthless or that you will never be or become anything. Avoid internalizing the negative opinion of others so that you can believe you are indeed the person God created you to be, regardless of their opinion and even your own doubt.

God created you and He did a great job. You will do great things.

Stay focused on God and His path and His plans. You are somebody—you are the somebody that God created!

God will show you some amazing things and will show you some amazing details about yourself. God will show up in some amazing ways in your life. God will do things you never imagined at the most awesome time in your life.

God will arrive within seconds of you quitting or doing other terrible things, proving that He is present in your life, available for you to access Him.

Invest in yourself the way God planned. Do the will of God so that God can reward you justly. There will be some rough times. Job can attest to that but God was faithful and kept Job. God will keep you in the best and worst of times.

God created you.

God created you with well-considered plans.

God created you to do awesome stuff.

You were planned. Not a mistake or accident or catastrophe.

You are the definition of purpose.

You are the purpose.

You have a purpose.

God loves you infinitely—without condition.

WEEK THREE REFLECTION

1. What do you think about the scriptures? What do they mean to you?

____

____

____

____

2. How did these scriptures change your thoughts and attitude about yourself?

____

____

____

____

3. Did this help you to reconsider the negative perception you had about yourself previously? How will your perception about yourself change?

____

____

____

____

4. Who are the negative people who need to be removed from your head?

____

____

5. What is your purpose? What do you want to be as an adult?

6. What are your dreams?

7. What do you think God wants you to do? How will you find out?

8. Who helps you to be positive and optimistic about your life? What does that person do? Why?

____

____

WEEK THREE PROJECT

1. Vision board. You will create a board about yourself and where you are headed. It is designed to keep you focused, especially when trouble is present and doubt surfaces.
    a. Picture of yourself
    b. Favorite scripture
    c. Dreams
    d. Goals
    e. Career choice
    f. Motivational quote
    g. An advocate (person who motivates, and helps you stay focused)

2. Take pictures of the vision board and post it to all of your social media sites, send to your family, friends, and to your advocate.

WEEK THREE JOURNAL

WEEK FOUR

God Forgives You

[13] Bear with each other and forgive one another if any of you has a grievance against someone. Forgive as the Lord forgave you.

Colossians 3:13

[25] And when you stand praying, if you hold anything against anyone, forgive them, so that your Father in heaven may forgive you your sins."

Mark 11:25

[9] If we confess our sins, he is faithful and just and will forgive us our sins and purify us from all unrighteousness.

1 John 1:9

You have cursed. Daily.

You have skipped class.

You have cheated on your assignments and tests.

You have lied.

You have had sex before marriage.

You have been disrespectful.

You have gossiped.

You have hurt someone's feelings.

You got pregnant.

You had the baby.

You had an abortion.

You tried to commit suicide.

You ran away.

You robbed someone.

You took drugs. You got high. Regularly.

You smoked cigarettes.

You drank alcohol.

You got drunk.

You shared someone else's secrets.

You acted like God abandoned you.

You are hard to love.

You cannot love others.

You have a hard time accepting God's love.

You have stolen.

You stabbed someone.

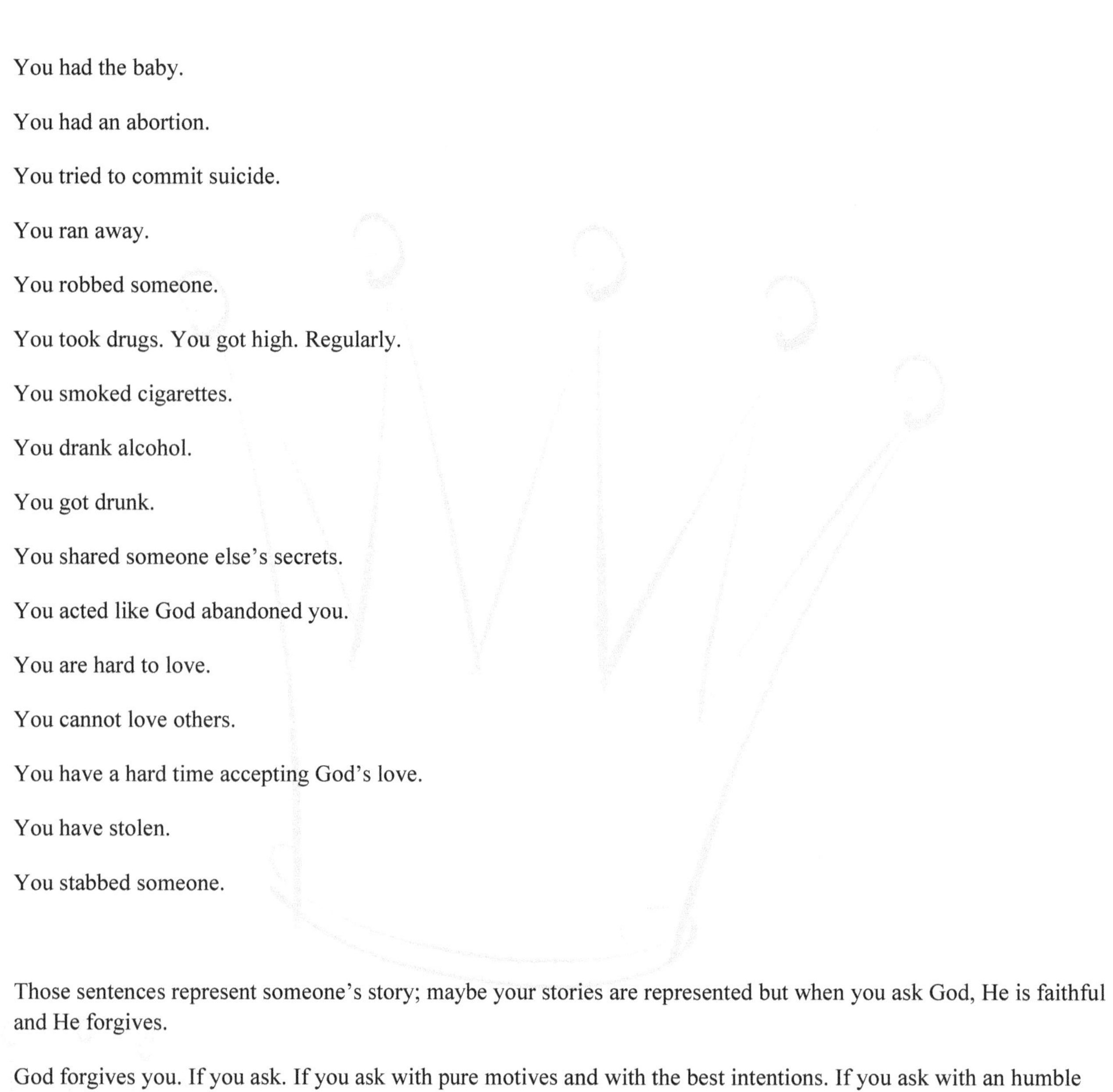

Those sentences represent someone's story; maybe your stories are represented but when you ask God, He is faithful and He forgives.

God forgives you. If you ask. If you ask with pure motives and with the best intentions. If you ask with an humble heart. If you ask without intention to ever do it again. If you forgive those who have offended you.

Your story is not unique. Your story is not new. You were not first to do or think any of these situations.

The best part is that God already knew it. God is not surprised by your actions. You still disappoint Him. He is prepared to forgive you anyway. His only requirement is that you also forgive others.

Well, He forgave you. Now forgive yourself! That may be the hardest part. If you are still reliving that moment, then you need to stop. If you keep reminding yourself of what you have done, you will not grow. You cannot progress. It is time to move forward despite what has happened.

Forgive yourself. It will lift you. It will lift your spirit.

Forgive Others

You were abandoned.

You were betrayed.

You were raped.

You were robbed.

You were adopted.

You were molested.

You were sold for drugs.

You were traded for alcohol.

You were prostituted to help support your family.

You were accused.

You took the blame for a crime so that some other family member could stay out of jail.

You were lied on.

You were cheated on.

You were humiliated.

These may not be part of your story but this is someone's story. You do not need to see it in writing because it is etched in your memory and on your soul. Forgive others so that you can be free. Forgive others that have wronged you. They will be surprised at that action because they would not forgive themselves in these same circumstances. They do not deserve your forgiveness. But in fact, neither do you. You don't deserve God's forgiveness, but God forgave you anyway.

It sounds simple and it is simple. FORGIVE. It is not easy. It is really difficult. In order to forgive, we assume that the hurt disappears. That is not true either. Forgiveness starts the healing process. Imagine how you will feel when you release that space in your mind and heart. It is liberating. There is a transfer of power when you forgive. You get it back—all the power returns to you. Imagine it: holding up your head again, loving again, smiling again, and all that goes with discontinuing the judgement of what happened to you which was out of your control.

Forgiveness is the truest part of this whole life. When you forgive, you submit to God and all that is attached to the situation also surrenders to God.

Forgive.

Be forgiven.

Be forgiving.

Be healed.

Be Free.

WEEK FOUR REFLECTION

1. Who do you need to forgive? Make a two-column list with the name of the person and the reason why you need to forgive them.

____

____

____

____

2. What do you need to be forgiven by God? By yourself?

____

____

____

____

3. What can you do to avoid needing forgiveness?

____

____

4. Who do you need to be forgiven by? How will you go about securing that forgiveness?

____

____

____

____

WEEK FOUR PROJECT

1. Write a letter to yourself, forgiving yourself.

2.   Write a letter to God, asking God for forgiveness.

3. Write a letter to someone you need to forgive. Who? Why? What happened? When will you forgive?

____

____

____

____

____

____

____

____

____

____

____

____

____

____

4. Write a letter to someone you need to be forgiven by.

WEEK FOUR JOURNAL

WEEK FIVE

God Hears You

Pray

[9] "This, then, is how you should pray:
"'Our Father in heaven, hallowed be your name,
[10] your kingdom come, your will be done, on earth as it is in heaven.
[11] Give us today our daily bread.
[12] And forgive us our debts, as we also have forgiven our debtors.
[13] And lead us not into temptation, but deliver us from the evil one.'
[14] For if you forgive other people when they sin against you, your heavenly Father will also forgive you.

Matthew 6:9-14

[44] But I tell you, love your enemies and pray for those who persecute you

Matthew 5:44

[28] bless those who curse you, pray for those who mistreat you.

Luke 6:28

[18] Again he prayed, and the heavens gave rain, and the earth produced its crops.

James 5:18

Prayer—it's what your mother and grandmother do!! Yes, that is true but it is also what you do or should start to do. Prayer is your personal conversation with God. Prayer is not your grocery list or shopping wish list. This conversation is where and when you disclose your whole heart and God is listening to your authentic petitions.

God is listening. He does not need you to be poetic or super spiritual. He does have some rules about prayer:

—be authentic, genuine, truthful

—be specific

—do not babble on and on: say just enough

—ask in Jesus' name

—remember to confess your sins and ask for forgiveness

—be thankful

—be gracious

—recognize God for His glory

Prayer is just a conversation. There is nothing to be afraid of. The prayer is a dialogue so listen for God's voice and the urgings of the Holy Spirit. God will speak to you. There is certain amount of fear with hearing God's voice. It really does not matter how many times you hear from God, you may feel some trepidation about hearing God's voice. That is understandable.

Please do also understand that just because God's voice or His message may be cause for trepidation, your personal feelings do not stop God from talking to you.

There is no way to suggest a way to be prepared for His voice or His message. His voice is inevitable so start getting prepared. Prayer is your tool to overcome such areas of fright.

The questions most often asked about prayer are:\

—what do I pray about?

Everything.

—When do I pray?

Daily and on all occasions.

—Who do I pray for?

Everyone, especially those who curse and persecute you.

—How do I pray?

Just a conversation. Not like talking casually with your friends or the disrespect you give your parents. There's not a formal format. Just talk to Him.

—Why pray?

You pray because you need to share and you need direction and you need answers. Only God can give you what you are seeking. You pray because God invites you to pray. You pray because the Holy Spirit was sent to intercede on our behalf according to the will of God.

—Where do you pray?

Everywhere and on every occasion. Sometimes you will need to pray out loud. Sometimes you will need to pray with your eyes open. Sometimes you will need to pray in your head because you are already talking. Sometimes you will need to pray in front of others. Sometimes you will need to pray but will not know what to pray.

Just pray.

WEEK FIVE REFLECTION

1. Who do you know that prays? Can you talk to them about their prayer life? Ask her/him all about their prayer life, such as when, why, how, who, where and what.

____

____

____

____

2. Do you pray? Are there any specific conditions under which you pray or do not pray? Why do you pray?

____

____

____

____

3. Do you pray with others? Who? Under what conditions?

____

____

____

____

4. Are you afraid to pray? Why or why not?

____

____

5. Do you pray for others? Who? Why do you pray for them?

6. Do people pray for you? Who?

7. Why do you pray?

8. What stops you from praying?

____

____

9.   What keeps you praying? Or what makes you stop?

____

____

____

10. What does prayer mean to you?

____

____

____

11. What age did you start recognizing prayer and its place in your life?

____

____

____

WEEK FIVE PROJECT

1. Make a list of people who pray: Prayer Warriors.

____

____

____

____

2. Make a list of your personal prayer requests.

____

____

____

____

____

____

____

3. Make a list of your prayer victories.

____

____

____

____

____

____

____

____

4.   Make a list of people you are praying for as well as what they are in need of.

____

____

____

____

____

____

5.   Do an internet search for famous prayers of comfort, adoration, peace and thanksgiving. List them below.

____

____

____

____

____

---

6. Schedule your prayer time, twice daily, on your calendar on your phone. Pray when the alarm sounds.

WEEK FIVE JOURNAL

WEEK SIX

God Expects Faith

[1]Now faith is the substance of things hoped for, the evidence of things not seen. [2]This is what the ancients were commended for.
[3]By faith we understand that the universe was formed at God's command, so that what is seen was not made out of what was visible.
[4]By faith Abel brought God a better offering than Cain did. By faith he was commended as righteous, when God spoke well of his offerings. And by faith Abel still speaks, even though he is dead.
[5]By faith Enoch was taken from this life, so that he did not experience death: "He could not be found, because God had taken him away." For before he was taken, he was commended as one who pleased God. [6]And without faith it is impossible to please God, because anyone who comes to him must believe that he exists and that he rewards those who earnestly seek him.

Hebrews 11:1-6 (KJV/NIV)

Faith is the evidence of what we hope for and the assurance of what we do not see. That's an advanced definition, so let's get basic. Faith is believing, without doubt, that God is real, that He will provide, that He hears you, and sees you, that God will give you the desires unless your desires sabotage the will of God.

Faith cannot come to pass if you do not work, you still have to study and memorize and work. Faith is not the scenario when you show up for test and expect to pass, but you have not paid attention in class, have not taken any notes, and you have neglected your homework; you have not even research the topic on the internet.

Faith is that you have paid attention in class, participated, studied every day. You get to the test and freeze. You are worried that you are going to forget everything. Faith is that you trust God to bring all that you have studied to come back to your memory. Faith is your hard work so apply for that position, even though you may not be as qualified as the other applicants, but you are awarded the position. God expects faith. The world tells you to doubt. Even those close to you may encourage you to doubt. But we can exercise our faith in all situations and circumstances.

Faith requires belief and actions. Study. Take the tests. Apply for colleges, trusting that you will be admitted and be financed. Work ethic and hard work is what faith is based on. Faith is you doing your part and trusting God for the rest.

Faith is hard and is not casual and is quite intentional. Faith is based on your relationship with God—how much do you trust them? How much do you trust Him? That's how much faith you have. Based on that, how much faith do you have? Do you have a little or a lot? Your faith had to be built, similar to lifting weights. This means you will be presented with opportunities to see the measure of your faith. There will be several events in your life which will help you expand and develop your faith.

You may have already experienced some of those events. A death in your family. An uninvolved parent. Hard school transitions. Incest. Molestation. Rape. Date rape. Bad break-up. This list is not comprehensive or conclusive. Your faith will be developed over time, through tests, events which cause you to ask God where He is and why does He feel so far away. There are Biblical persons who were tested by God and lived to tell about it.

Job lost his children and his property and his wealth. This was later revealed that his faith was tested. After his faith passed his test, he was gifted with more children, more money, double the cattle and other livestock, and the same wife.

Hannah wanted a child. She promised God the child. She promised with and unyielding faith that other women can only hope to model with the same zeal and authenticity.

Mary thought her reputation would be ruined and that she would not be able to ever marry, yet she in fact birthed Jesus Christ.

Sarah got ahead of God and His promise when she arranged a birth of a son with her husband and someone else, so when she actually conceived and birthed Isaac, she wondered how her faith became so faint and weak.

David sinned and the product of that sin was taken from him and Bathsheba. David fasted for seven days but when God took their son, David ended the fast, reunited with Bathsheba, at which point they conceived Solomon. Solomon was the evidence of the promises that God made.

So there are many others which you can study in Hebrews 11.

Will you be labeled faithful? Or unfaithful? Will you be faithful during easier and the hardest times?

God expects you to stay close to Him. And faith is necessary to please God.

God expects faith.

WEEK SIX REFLECTION

1. Who do you know that has faith? How did you determine that they were faithful?

____

____

____

____

2. Do you consider yourself faithful?

____

____

____

3. What is your definition of faith?

____

____

____

4. Can you recall a time when you were faithful? Share the situation.

____

____

____

5. How will you improve your faithfulness?

____

____

____

____

6. Who will you share your faith with?

____

____

____

____

7. Who will you encourage to have faith?

____

____

____

____

8. How would God grade your faith?

____

____

____

9. Has there ever been a cost to your unfaithfulness?

10. Whose faith are you modeling your faith after?

WEEK SIX PROJECT

1. Start a journal, mostly to pray, to praise God and keep record or your faith moments.

2. Find 15 scriptures about faith outside of Hebrews.

3.   Write a letter to God expressing your philosophy of faith.

4. Write a letter to encourage someone close to you to keep their faith intact.

WEEK SIX JOURNAL

WEEK SEVEN

God Gifts You

[6] We have different gifts, according to the grace given to each of us. If your gift is prophesying, then prophesy in accordance with your faith; [7] if it is serving, then serve; if it is teaching, then teach; [8] if it is to encourage, then give encouragement; if it is giving, then give generously; if it is to lead, do it diligently; if it is to show mercy, do it cheerfully.

Romans 12:6-8

[4] There are different kinds of gifts, but the same Spirit distributes them. [5] There are different kinds of service, but the same Lord. [6] There are different kinds of working, but in all of them and in everyone it is the same God at work. [7] Now to each one the manifestation of the Spirit is given for the common good. [8] To one there is given through the Spirit a message of wisdom, to another a message of knowledge by means of the same Spirit, [9] to another faith by the same Spirit, to another gifts of healing by that one Spirit, [10] to another miraculous powers, to another prophecy, to another distinguishing between spirits, to another speaking in different kinds of tongues, and to still another the interpretation of tongues. [11] All these are the work of one and the same Spirit, and he distributes them to each one, just as he determines.

1 Corinthians 12:4-11

Your voice. Your hands. Your mind. Your time. Your financial resources. You were given all of these things because you are trusted with that gift to share it with other.

God gives each of us at least one gift. God gave us that gift to use to benefits His glory. Not for any other reason, but to give Him glory and to serve those who He sent to sever for His glory.

Gifts are details that you are good at because of His decision.

In 1 Corinthians 12:4-11, Paul speaks of gifts which God gives to each of us. We also need to use our gifts in concert with other Christians and to unify the body of Christ.

Your gifts cannot be given back or traded or replaced. Your gifts are to be used as God requires, when God requires, and to whom He requires to be the beneficiary of those gifts. God gave you those gifts to use—not to sit on or just simply ignore or try to forget it or act like it doesn't exist or act like God was not talking to you.

It is not beneficial so do not whine to God that you do not want that particular gift or you wish for someone's gift. These gifts are special for each one of us and are to be used at His specified time, so trading and whining and coveting are all irresponsible requests.

Asking for someone else's gifts is coveting. Not a wise choice at all.

Now about the gifts to be used for people when you do not want to. Because these gifts are God—issued, you do not get a choice of who you serve with those gifts. Once we understand that God is not selfish so we cannot be either, then we will understand why we have to serve others who we may not like do not know and cannot understand.

There is then the responsibility of giving credit to God for those gifts and not taking credit yourself. God is the orchestrator of these gifts and all that is associated with it. You have been the beneficiary of the gifts of others. You have heard prayers, and some you didn't hear. You have heard songs, thousands of them. That talent is from God. God expect that those voices will bring Him glory. Many people envy great singers, but there is usually a battle within those singers about whether to sing secular music versus gospel, based on the assumed financial differential.

In that scripture text, there are some serious gifts which are given: healer, preacher, teacher, and miraculous powers to name a few.

If you are gifted with the ability of healing, then you may have to heal someone who just insulted you or who does not like you. That is God's expectation.

That is why we need to consider the life of Christ when Jesus put the ear of the soldier which Peter had cut off. This is the same soldier who had falsely accused Jesus and was there to make sure that the Jesus died. Jesus was staring one of His enemies in the face and still fixed the ear. Most of us would have kept walking away, the displaced ear and its possible outcomes. Well, we are not Jesus but daily we strive to be more and more like Him. Keep the gifts in perspective.

Use them or lose them. This idea is one which could be argued but do understand that if you don't use them for God, then you will not be successful using them in the secular community.

"Your gifts will make room for you." Wisdom comes with waiting and waiting builds knowledge and perseverance.

You will learn to use your gift while you wait. You will develop an audience for your gifts. You will seek reasons to save others. Also seek others which have the same or similar gift so that you can have a mentor and wise counsel for the best use and service of your gift.

Your unselfish use of your gifts makes you free and keeps you whole. When you give freely of your gifts, then you have pleased God. You can live without guilt or unrest.

God blesses your obedience. He will bless your efforts.

Study your gifts. Study others when God gave them the same gifts. Study God so that you will understand His moves. And what He expects your moves to be.

The parable of the talents is one worth mentioning here. Matthew 25:14-30. The lesson of the parable is that when God gives you something, He expects you to use it. Don't bury or neglect it.

WEEK SEVEN REFLECTION

1. What are your gifts? What excuse(s) do you use to avoid being obedient? You do not know how God will multiply or manifest your gifts through your obedience.

2. What are your talents? What is your favorite gift of your gift(s)?

3. Why are you afraid to use your gifts and talents? When do you plan to use them for God as He intended?

4. What does God want you to do? How do you know? Why do you think God gave that gift/talent?

____

____

5. What will you do differently now that you know what your gifts are intended to do?

____

____

____

____

6. Who will you share with for gift mentoring? Who will you share your gifts with? Are you reluctant to share? Why? Are you scared to exercise your gift(s)? Why? How can we overcome that reluctancy and that fear?

____

____

____

____

7. What are your parent's gifts?

____

____

____

____

8. What friend(s) will you share about your gifts and theirs? What will you share? Do they know their gifts? Will you help them to discover their gifts?

WEEK SEVEN PROJECT

1. Take a Spiritual Gift Inventory. Email the results to your parent(s), mentor, your church family, and yourself.

www.spiritualgifttest.com

2. Research the results of the test and seek to apply it to your church to see where you can serve at your church.

3. Research the results of the test to seek areas of the community and your school where you can serve.

WEEK SEVEN JOURNAL

WEEK EIGHT

Sex and Intimate Relationships

But since sexual immorality is occurring, each man should have sexual relations with his own wife, and each woman with her own husband.

1 Corinthians 7:2

Puberty is not kind because it stimulates within you hormones and body changes which you may not understand and you definitely did not get a warning that it would result in this.

Sex has become THE topic of conversation. It is everywhere. In every song. In very movie. In every television show. In everything. Everywhere. Then the adults say don't have sex, don't look too sexy, and don't ask any sex related questions. When teenagers start asking sex questions, adults get uncomfortable. Adults will assume that you are asking because you are planning to have sex.

The Bible said not to have sex until you are married.

There are some reasons why not to have sex:

1. Because God said not to.
2. When you are married and have no experience, neither of you will have anything to compare the experience to, so there is no issue about a past which inevitably comes up as a bad thing in future relationships.
3. There is no judgement that can be rendered when your answer to how many partners is 0. When you answer with certain numbers, then you are judged based on the subjective nature of that number at the age when you are asked. For example, 3 partners by age 18 is too many versus 3 partners by age 40 is 'okay.' These numbers are subjective and judgmental but God only intended for you to have one partner your whole life.
4. You will not have anyone to compare the experience to so that your experience can be free of judgement. You cannot covet or wish for something you have never had. You will not be able to compare your husband to your first partner, and this lack of comparison will cause you to enjoy your partner without prejudice.

5. You do not have to worry about disease or pregnancy; both of which can stay with you for the rest of your life.
6. If you are going to regret your partner sharing what happened, then don't do it.
7. If you cannot talk about your decision with everyone you know, then don't do it.
8. Are you going to be embarrassed about the act? Then don't do it.
9. Are you going to be uncomfortable telling your child what age you first had sex? If not, then don't do it.
10. How are you going to feel about getting caught in the act?
11. What happens if your friend's family no longer allows you to be friends with each other because you are not a good influence because you had sex?
12. What if your partner does not treat you well? What if you don't enjoy the experience?
13. What if your partner is not committed to you and you thought he was?

These thirteen reasons are enough to not to, but you can also think of others.

Sex is not all that you can do to be intimate. Intimacy needs to be managed and entered into sparingly and cautiously. Intimacy is a mental, physical, and emotional closeness which needs to be considered the step just before sex because it usually leads to sex.

What are you defining as intimacy? Why is intimacy important at this age? Why is it important now? What is the need to be intimate at this time? What do you intend to achieve when you become intimate? What does intimacy mean for the relationship?

What are you saving for your husband? If you have sex as a teenager, and you are intimate with all of your boyfriends, then what are you saving for your husband? How will he feel special and set apart? All decisions are final and there are no 'take-backs.' Once you have sex, you cannot undo or rewind or change the fact you have already done that. So this decision needs to be made very carefully and very wisely, because you cannot change it once it's made.

Sex had forever emotional implications. Also it is someone who you will be attached to whether good or bad for the rest of your life. Is this someone you want a lifetime emotional and mental attachment? Will that attachment interrupt your marriage? Will that memory linger in your mind and heart causing you not to be able to focus in your marriage?

Why is sex so important right now? What are you in a hurry for? What does having sex say about or do for the relationship? Can the relationship really support having sex?

What are other people at your school or your church going to say when they find out? How are you going to feel when they find out?

It is important to protect your reputation as well as your emotional and mental health.

Finally, sex is a commitment. Do you and your mate view it the same? Do you consider the commitment the same? What happens if the partner does not feel that same way? What happens if that partner violates the commitment and decides to also have sex with someone else? How are you going to feel? What will you do? How will you recover?

Sex and the decision to engage in a sexual relationship is a big deal—one you cannot enter into lightly.

How will he treat you after the initial encounter?

WEEK EIGHT REFLECTION

1. What is sex as you define it?

____

____

____

____

2. Who do you know that is having sex? How long have they been having sex? How long have you known? Have they had more than one partner since they have been having sex?

____

____

____

____

3. Do you want to have sex? Why? Do your friends/media/others have a greater influence?

____

____

____

4. With whom do you want to have sex? Why? Does this person want to have sex with you?

____

____

5. When is an appropriate time to have sex? Can you wait until you are married to have sex? Why or why not?

6. Why is sex so important to you? To others? Why is it important right now?

7. When are you considering having sex? Today? Tomorrow? This week? Next week? Next month? Next 6 months? Next year?

8. What will it take for you to wait? What will it 'cost' for you to wait?

____

____

9. Why does the Bible say to wait until you are married to have sex?

____

____

____

____

10. What would you do if you became pregnant? Have the child? Abortion? Adoption? How long will that choice and consequence last? How will you endure/survive this consequence?

____

____

____

____

11. Do you know/understand that your parent(s) is graded on your behavior and outcome, so if you are pregnant or have the reputation for having sex, then it makes them look bad? Do you know/understand that they will be embarrassed? Do you know/understand that it will make them look like did not parent correctly?

____

____

____

12. Does how you feel about yourself—your self-esteem—determine your ability to say no to having sex?

____

____

____

____

WEEK EIGHT PROJECT

1. Write out a description of how you 'dream' the encounter will be.

____

____

____

____

2. Ask 5 people about her first experience.
    a.   Was it worth it?
    b.   Do you regret it?
    c.   Do you still replay the encounter in your mind?
    d.   What advice do you have for me?

____

____

____

____

3. Make a list of behavior and activities which create intimacy but does not involve touching. Please include conversation topics. Please include how long you can do each activity.

____

____

____

____

WEEK EIGHT JOURNAL

WEEK NINE

God Gives Wisdom Through Experience

[1] The proverbs of Solomon son of David, king of Israel:
[2] for gaining wisdom and instruction;
for understanding words of insight;
[3] for receiving instruction in prudent behavior,
doing what is right and just and fair;
[4] for giving prudence to those who are simple,
knowledge and discretion to the young—
[5] let the wise listen and add to their learning,
and let the discerning get guidance—
[6] for understanding proverbs and parables,
the sayings and riddles of the wise.
[7] The fear of the LORD is the beginning of knowledge,
but fools despise wisdom and instruction.

Proverbs 1:1-7

Wisdom is defined as knowledge of what is true or right coupled with just judgement as to action. Wisdom is synonymous with common sense, insight and discernment.

Wisdom requires action which means that you do the best thing based on your options. Wisdom will also call for you to select no option when taking action is detrimental to you and others. Wisdom is demonstrated through your words and deeds. So how do you choose wisdom, when is it available, and how will you demonstrate that your wisdom is present?

Wisdom is ongoing—He adds to it daily and He does so because we ask for wisdom and you also have some experiences which also grows you into some wisdom. Wisdom means that if you made a mistake, then you do not repeat that same error. Wisdom means that you study and research what to do next time when that situation happens again.

Wisdom also dictates your speech. As a teenager, you are tempted to say something disrespectful and unproductive. Your words challenged your parent and her response was surprising. You are still surprised at what she did and said. Wisdom teaches you to never challenge her in that manner ever again.

Wisdom will speak logically for the best for you and your future. 'Think before you speak' has often been said but it is rarely completely explained. Think (before you speak) of the consequences of your words before you say them. The consequences include the feelings of the others or the impact of your words on another person's mentality. Think about what your words will mean to others or how it will make the other person feel. Think about what you are committed to once you speak. Thinking about what message you want to send helps you to deliver that message with compassion and love, kindness and grace. Wisdom offers you the opportunity to see the message the way the other person will receive it.

Wisdom is priceless. And unique. Wisdom helps you remain calm. Wisdom keeps you focused and focused on what really matters. Wisdom prevents you from saying ugly words to others, preventing them from feeling good about themselves.

Wisdom also helps you to be silent when appropriate and necessary.

Wisdom shows up at different times and because of that, we will never stop receiving wisdom. Now you have wisdom to help you to successfully survive your childhood. Wisdom keeps your pictures from the cloud, off of the internet, and out of the hands of the enemy which would cause harm to your future.

Use this wisdom to save yourself and your peers and your family and strangers who cross your path from the very foolish choices, which could end your ability to continue to make choices. Your poor choices will keep you from graduating, going to college, living a free life, or to continue to live at all.

You may be asking how to receive wisdom. The answer is easy: Ask. Asking God for wisdom is all that you have to do. God will give you wisdom just because you asked. The next question should be 'how do I know when I have received the wisdom I requested.' Well that is distinguished by your words, your dress, your attitude, your decisions, and your activities.

Wisdom is being obedient to your parents when you don't want to do your chores.

Wisdom is completing your homework and studying for exams, especially when you don't feel like it. You are wise enough to understand that your grades affect **your** future, not your teachers or your parents. So when you are not wise enough to do your homework or study for tests or ask questions in class or go the extra mile for yourself.

Wisdom is listening to others for the information you need to be successful. Listen to those around you. If you question the information, please ask someone you trust about the information you have received. Wisdom is not cheating on tests and assignments. Wisdom is not having sex. Wisdom is not having sex without protection. Wisdom is listening to the advice of your friends when they risk your friendship to keep you from being hurt when they see that boyfriend with another girl.

Wisdom is going to church and worship and praise and pray and confess and tithe and fellowship. Wisdom tells the truth. Wisdom is being where you are supposed to be when you are driving the car after you have received your license. Wisdom is from God. It is to be used so that you recognize God and stop making the regular mistakes, which wisdom will cause you to avoid.

WEEK NINE REFLECTION

1. Define wisdom. How did you reach that definition?

____

____

____

____

2. Who do you know who is wise? When did you reach that decision?

____

____

____

____

3. When did you first ask to be wise?

____

____

____

____

4. Share three examples of when you have acted wisely.

____

____

____

5. Share three examples of when you acted without the benefit of wisdom, but the next time when the similar event happened, you responded wisely.

6. How do you share your wisdom with others?

7. Among your age group, who do you consider to be wise? Why?

8. List the top10 scriptures listed as a result of a search for wisdom in biblegateway.com or the Bible on your phone. Read them. Select one that you can memorize.

WEEK NINE PROJECT

1. Make a list of 15 wise Bible characters.

____

____

____

____

____

____

2. Make a list of 15 wise people you know personally.

____

____

____

____

____

____

3. Create postcards of the scriptures you researched in the questions.

WEEK NINE JOURNAL

WEEK TEN

Study and Meditation

[1] Blessed is the one who does not walk in step with the wicked
or stand in the way that sinners take or sit in the company of mockers,
[2] but whose delight is in the law of the LORD, and who meditates on his law day and night.
[3] That person is like a tree planted by streams of water, which yields its fruit in season
and whose leaf does not wither—whatever they do prospers.
[4] Not so the wicked! They are like chaff that the wind blows away.
[5] Therefore the wicked will not stand in the judgment, nor sinners in the assembly of the righteous.
[6] For the LORD watches over the way of the righteous, but the way of the wicked leads to destruction.

Psalm 1

[15] Do your best to present yourself to God as one approved, a worker who does not need to be ashamed and who correctly handles the word of truth.

2 Timothy 2:15

[15] I meditate on your precepts and consider your ways.

Psalm 119:15

Study will be best done through reading, asking questions, and using commentaries to understand the scriptures. Further, asking the Holy Spirit for guidance about the words and His message. Taking notes will be a part of studying as well.

As a teenager, you are busy and have built-in "excuses" for not having time to study or read the Bible. However, you need to make time to study and read the Bible. You can start with the scriptures in this book, and there are additional ones in the appendix.

There are several reasons why study is important:

♦   Closer relationship with God

♦   Better understanding of God

- Better understanding of what God's wants

- Freedom to hear God's voice

- Able to share God with others

- Know your source for hope and strength in times of trouble

Closer Relationship to God

As you grow up, you will question where God is and what He is dong and how He wants you to behave and respond. This relationship, your relationship with God will grow because of the time that you spend with God.

Consider the time you spend on social media and with your friends—that is how those relationships grow: TIME.

God and you will became closer because of time you dedicate to God. Nobody grows a relationship telepathically or just because you think about the relationship of because you want to or because you are supposed to have a relationship. Relationships grow because of time spent and knowledge exchanged.

A closer relationship will yield a level of comfort and develops the dependency you can grow accustomed to from God. This closer relationship is based on what you do so that God can respond.

A closer relationship will help you hear from God. In a relationship, you usually listen to the One you are in a relationship with. This closer relationship will also afford you the ability to hear God. A closer relationship will hopefully stop you from doubting God. Relationships develop with trust and love and contact.

But you will want to be close to God at your darkest hours but you cannot get there only in concept or request, so it is not instant. Without working at the development of the relationship, you cannot experience the closeness that you desire and without that work, you cannot appreciate the closeness and the privilege that the closeness affords you. If you did not work on it, you would not know when you had arrived at closeness. Do you know how long it took to get close enough to your best friend, in order to call her/him your best friend; in order for her/him to call you best friend? Well you can see what is required to become close to someone, then there is God. The path to closeness to God is different, but time is still required.

You want to get close to Him now, so that you will not be asking Him where He is, or rather where you are, when your world is shaken, either ever so slightly or earthquake-like.

You want to be close to your Creator, mostly because He loves you and your closeness demonstrates the reciprocity of your love.

Better Understanding of God

When you are reading the Bible, you are hearing and seeing the thoughts and desires, the commands and covenants of God. This study will cause you to understand God, which causes you to understand yourself better.

Your investment is reflective of your desire to understand. This is the same God who you will ask for blessings, demand help, blame for your misfortune, and pray for healing, so you need to understand Him and His ways.

There will be times and events which cause you to ask God why did He do something. As you read and study, you will begin to understand God better so when you ask now, you ask with the perspective and understanding.

There are times when you want to know and understand God so that you can better understand your path.

When you start to question God, you will study others who have questioned God and what their experience was when they questioned God.

Better Understanding of What God Wants

When you meet people for the first time, you start getting to know them. You become familiar with their ways, thoughts, and mannerisms. You do this through time and observation. So with God, you will do something similar. Studying will show you what God wants. God answers questions and concerns about love, forgiveness, honor, deceit, leadership, sex, temptation, how to escape temptation, pains, fear, death, faith, and about one thousand other topics and situations. The Holy Spirit also illuminates the message God wants to you to receive when you are reading. The Holy Spirit will share with you the actual event that relates to the scriptures so that you can apply them immediately.

Psalm 119:19 reads, 'I have hidden Your word in my heart so that I may not sin against Thee.' In order to do that you have to actually have that word in your heart, which comes by studying and working toward an understanding. The other caveat here is that scripture can mean something different in different situations. The scripture, does not change, rather how you see it being applied.

You also want to know that God has not forgotten you or dismissed your situation.

Why should God send a 'new' word to your rather regular situation? If your situation has already been addressed, then you should read how God addresses it so that you can apply that to your situation. God addressed what to do in adversity, after sinning, when you don't know how to pray, amongst others so clearly that we don't need to ask for certain things—He has already provided us with that.

What He wants is ALL that matters—God's will BE done.

Freedom to Hear God's Voice

One of the most asked questions is 'how do I know when God is speaking to me?' Again: relationship. That is the first question is do you have a relationship with God so you can hear form God. There is one such story about Jesus talking to someone with whom He did not have a relationship. Without a relationship, you will recognize neither His voice nor His words.

Saul (Acts 9) was walking down the road when Jesus called to him saying, 'Saul, Saul, why do you persecute Me?' Well as you can imagine Saul was scared but Jesus was intent on Saul understanding who He was so the next few steps were very interesting.

Hearing God's voice requires action, so be careful asking for Him to speak.

When God speaks, He is clear and profound and decisive. Your decision to 'hear' and 'listen' needs to be started with an understanding that you may hear something you don't want to hear and some things you certainly don't want to do. If you ask then be prepared for what He says. Then do what He says.

Because you have a relationship and you can hear Him, then refrain from asking 'why me?' 'Why me?' is an easy question, but the answer is mighty and powerful.

God's response sounds like, "Why not you?" Then God follows that up with, "Because this is My will for your life—the life I created. So I chose you to do some things that fulfill My will. I did not chose you according to your personal desires or what others say or think of your capabilities or worthiness." Finally, God may also suggest that you stop asking Him that and maybe even other questions. Review Job 38-41. God asks Job questions for 129, one hundred twenty nine, verses. For 129 verses, Job was listening intently with no positive response. What can you say when God asks you over 100 questions?

Once you read the verses, you too will understand why questioning God is not necessary nor a good idea.

Keep listening with the expectations that God is answering your prayers and your questions.

Able to Share God with Others

This relationship with God will cause several things to happen. The first of which is that others will see this change and will ask you what is going on with you, giving you the best opportunity to share God and Jesus with others. Don't miss this opportunity to say what God has done in your life and how your relationship has grown.

The second of which is that you will want to share with God with others because how your perspective has changed. This is growth and you certainly want to share that growth.

The relationship builds confidence in being able to share so it does not feel so awkward. Your confidence will influence others to do the same. Now that you know more you will be able to share more and help others to understand and answer questions they may have.

Know Your Source of Strength in Times of Trouble

When you were born, you were introduced to your mother by being laid on her chest. She was known for being your protection immediately. She was not questioned or tested; she was not auditioned or tried. For the most part, she still holds that same level.

So because of Mom, you know what protection looks like, so does God's protection and provision warrant/deserve questioning, testing, auditioning or trying? God gave you to your mother. He trusted her to protect and provide for you.

God can be trusted to protect you.

God is also your Source of strength when trouble comes. Trouble is defined as low grades, parent's divorcing, custody fights, suicidal thoughts, suicidal behaviors, relationship issues, family deaths, not making the team in a sport or activity, or anything else that you can think of or consider trouble.

There are troubling statistics about teen drug usage, teen overdose, teen sex, teen sexually transmitted diseases, teen pregnancy, teen suicide attempts, teen medical treatments for mental and emotional illnesses, teen suicide, teen dropouts, teen runaways, and teen alcoholism. These along with the remarkable rates of poverty and the new issues with human trafficking and teen prostitution, these are all aspects which cause concern for you as a teen, but especially a girl. These events need to drive you back to God. Through <u>all</u> things your Source is God—not drugs, sex, alcohol, and especially suicide. None of these can help you to overcome these issues like God has and always will be your Source in troubled times. ALL of those other issues will cause you more trouble.

Seek God—unashamedly!

Meditate is defined as continued or extended thought, reflection and contemplation. Meditating on God's word means to reflect on what you have read and on what God and the Holy Spirit has said. So after study, then there is meditation. Spend some quality time with God.

WEEK TEN REFLECTION

1. What time will you set aside to read God's word?

____

____

____

____

2. Do you have the Bible app on your phone so that you can read the Bible on the bus or other times when you are waiting?

____

____

____

____

3. Do you have a study partner or someone you can talk to about the Bible who is your age?

____

____

____

____

4. Do you have an adult/mentor who you can ask questions of about the Bible?

____

____

____

____

5. Do you know what a commentary is? Biblegateway.com has one that is useful.

____

____

____

____

6. What do you expect to gain by studying God's word?

____

____

____

____

7. What do you think will be the obstacle for studying and meditating? How will you overcome those obstacles?

____

____

____

____

WEEK TEN PROJECT

1. Download the Bible application of your choice on your phone and all of your electronic devices.

2. Share with your friends that you downloaded the app(s).

3. Put a schedule reminder in your phone for the time you will be spending reading the Bible. 15 minutes to start for 30 days. Progress to 30 minutes in 60 days.

4. Find a journal to write your scriptures that you read, your summary of those scriptures, and questions you have, any application you can make of those scriptures, and what you have learned. Also figure out how you will label your favorite scriptures. Also, how you will learn the favorite scriptures.

WEEK TEN JOURNAL

AIN'T I A WOMAN

Sojourner Truth

That man over there say
a woman needs to be helped into carriages
and lifted over ditches
and to have the best place everywhere.
Nobody ever helped me into carriages
or over mud puddles
or gives me a best place. . .

And ain't I a woman?
Look at me
Look at my arm!
I have plowed and planted
and gathered into barns
and no man could head me. . .
And ain't I a woman?
I could work as much
and eat as much as a man--
when I could get to it--
and bear the lash as well
and ain't I a woman?
I have born 13 children
and seen most all sold into slavery
and when I cried out a mother's grief
none but Jesus heard me. . .
and ain't I a woman?
that little man in black there say
a woman can't have as much rights as a man
cause Christ wasn't a woman
Where did your Christ come from?
From God and a woman!
Man had nothing to do with him!

If the first woman God ever made
was strong enough to turn the world
upside down, all alone
together women ought to be able to turn it
right-side up again.

"There is no exact copy of this speech given at the Women's rights Convention in Akron, Ohio, in 1852. The speech is adapted to the poetic format by Erelene Stetson from the copy found in Sojourner, *God's Faithful Pilgrim* by Arthur Huff Fauset, (Chapel Hill: University of North Carolina Press, 1938)."
The poem and note, along with other great women's poems, can be found in *Ain't I a Woman: A Book of Women's Poetry from Around The World,* Illona Linthwaite, Editor. New York: Wing Books, 1993, page 129.

WEEK ELEVEN

In Times of Trouble

[14] if my people, who are called by my name, will humble themselves and pray and seek my face and turn from their wicked ways, then I will hear from heaven, and I will forgive their sin and will heal their land.

2 Chronicle 7:14 (2 Chronicle 7:11-22)

God defines trouble differently from you. Trouble to the average human being is not as big or horrible as originally thought. Your trouble is not bigger than our God.

Even though the definitions are different, it does not stop the defining as trouble. Well consider your feeble list.

Short list:

- Pregnancy
- Family death
- Low grades
- Not admitted into college you prefer
- Your partner broke up with you or vice versa

God defines trouble differently. He sees trouble as succumbing to the enemy without seeking Him, not praying, not believing in Him, Jesus and the Holy Spirit, doubting and disbelieving Him, and blaspheming His name. Other than that, God can see you through everything else.

You may hear the statement: "Your trouble is not bigger than God." Initially, you may look skeptical at the statement and internally ask yourself, 'how is that possible? My mother is going to kill me.' Then you consider the shame that you have to endure because of your situation. You may even consider the consequences. But God knows all of that already and He knew what you would do it. The easiest activity is to avoid the activity which leads to your mother almost 'killing' you, embarrassment, shame, or condemnation, and the inconvenience of the situation.

Now, the other side is the preventative measure: go to God first before all of the other methods and mechanisms.

In life, people develop go-to's, like music, drugs, sex, shopping, to name a few. The caution that needs to be considered is that these 'go-to's' lead you away from God and cause temptation to become sin, again causing distance between you and God.

Escapes are understandable until they distance you from God or cause you to sin.

Seek God first. Easier said than done? True, but it also means that you have to be focused on God to make that happen.

Trouble does not last always.

WEEK ELEVEN REFLECTION

1. How can you stay out of trouble? What will it take to stay out of trouble?

____

____

____

____

2. What are your 'go-to's'? Which one(s) will you need to eliminate or modify so that you do not increase the distance between you and God?

____

____

____

____

3. Can you seek God on all occasions? If not, when will you start?

____

____

____

____

WEEK ELEVEN PROJECT

1. Make a list of scriptures which address the following topics:

    a. Temptation ____

    b. Sin ____

    c. Sex before marriage ____

    d. Alcohol____

    e. Drugs ____

    f. Forgiveness ____

2. Make a list of how you will avoid these temptations.

____

____

____

____

WEEK ELEVEN JOURNAL

WEEK TWELVE

Follow the One that Counts: Jesus

Leadership, Image, Reputation

[26] Then God said, "Let us make mankind in our image, in our likeness, so that they may rule over the fish in the sea and the birds in the sky, over the livestock and all the wild animals, and over all the creatures that move along the ground."
[27] So God created mankind in his own image, in the image of God he created them; male and female he created them.

Genesis 1:26-27

[25] "Therefore I tell you, do not worry about your life, what you will eat or drink; or about your body, what you will wear. Is not life more than food, and the body more than clothes?

Matthew 6:25

[18] As Jesus was walking beside the Sea of Galilee, he saw two brothers, Simon called Peter and his brother Andrew. They were casting a net into the lake, for they were fishermen. [19] "Come, follow me," Jesus said, "and I will send you out to fish for people." [20] At once they left their nets and followed him.

Matthew 4:18-20

Romans 8:29	Luke 6:27-28
James 3:9-10	John 15:18
Luke 21:17 (13-17)	Matthew 14:29a (14:25-33)
Galatians 1:23-24	John 8:7

As a teenager, you are invited to follow God daily. It is called peer pressure. 1 Timothy 4:12 reads: "Don't let anyone look down on you because you are young, but set an example for the believers in speech, in conduct, in love and in purity." Jesus calls you to be the leader He gifted you to be. There's a leader and follower within each of us. The point is that you need to remember when to use each of those roles.

Leadership of others to Jesus is following Jesus. Matthew 4:18-20 tells how Jesus selected His first disciples. Quite a story. Jesus has selected you as well. Who first introduced you to Christ? What is your testimony? Who have you shared that testimony with?

Jesus showed you how to lead when He walked up to the fishermen. He did it again when He gathered them to go to teach others. He did it again when He performed miracles. He did it again when crowds follow Him while He preached, because He taught the Word of God. He taught leadership when He expected those disciples then and His disciples (us) now to do exactly what He had done and do that for others. Jesus got upset with the disciples because they lacked the faith to do what He had already equipped them to do. Luke 9:1-6, Mark 8:34-38, and Mark 9:16-23.

Luke 9:1-6 tells how Jesus sent out the Twelve. So with these instructions at hand, we are called to follow Jesus, so what does your following and your leadership look like?

Leadership is an activity which needs others to follow Jesus. Also, doing whatever Jesus assigned you to do.

Leadership is the example you set before others as you follow Jesus and His instructions. You share Jesus with others so that they can empower others to do the same. You use your God-given gifts for God. You have faith that cause others to wonder how that is possible especially at your age. You use your gifts to elevate the kingdom and others expectedly respond. Leadership is praying when you really want to quit. You seek God and wait for His voice despite the fact that the situation looks bleak.

Leadership is being able to say no when temptation presents itself. Being able to walk away from those situations that could so easily entangle you.

<u>Image</u>

Genesis 1:26-27 (NIV)

What is your definition of image? God created you in His image. What is your image of God? Holy? Righteous? Forgiving? Loving? Gracious? Merciful? Powerful? Wise? Creative? You are most of that. And you can be all of that. You can simple make the decision to do so. When the simple decision does not make it happen, then you can ask God for what you lack.

God created you in His image. With that in mind, is what you are doing and look like supportive of that image? Is God pleased with your look and your attitude and your overall disposition? Does God care about how you look? Yes or no. No, God does not care if you wear designer clothes. In fact, in Matthew 6:25, the scripture tells you not to worry about what you will wear, that your body is more important than clothes. God does not care about the newest tennis shoes or the latest fashions.

God does care about how you wear the clothes you have. Is that skirt a respectable length? Or can your panties be seen when you bend over ever so slightly because the skirt is so short? Is your makeup so heavy that you look like a totally different person and nearly unrecognizable when you are not wearing any? Does your hair style vary so drastically that people do not recognize you? From week to week? Do you really need weave in your hair? What is wrong with God's original design? God made you with that length and grade of hair. You need to work on accepting God's unique work.

Your presentation of yourself is important and should be representative of God. Does your attire embarrass your family? Do you change clothes after you leave home because your mother/parents will not approve of what you want to wear?

With the hair, make-up, clothes and all, who are you trying to impress? Why? What is the benefit of impressing them? What is the point of making them think some uncomplimentary thoughts about you? When do you think that you will regret this image? Do you want to be known for this for the next 25 years? Are you okay with your daughter wearing the same outfit when she is a teenager? What will your grandmother and mother say if they see you in those clothes? What if your mother wore the clothes you want to wear?

<u>Reputation</u>

What do people think of you? How do you know? What is a good reputation? How would you maintain that good reputation? What does it take to renew that reputation? How long do you think it takes to recover from something which damaged your reputation?

Jesus was accused of some interesting events, but nothing that He could not recover from. Are you able to say the same?

You know girls who are known for having sex with boys who share their personal information with others. You know girls who do drugs. You know girls who drink. And get drunk. You know girls who do not study. You know girls who cheat in school. What do people say about those girls? What do you say about those girls? Are you one of those girls? How do you feel for those girls when people talk about them?

Why is your reputation important? Why is a good reputation important?

Let's examine reputation. It is what you are known for. You get to choose the nature of your reputation: great or horrible. Your behavior dictates your reputation. What you do and the choices you make are the determinants of this reputation. Protect your reputation at all costs.

No sex. It is amazing that girls are always the ones whose reputations falter for having sex. The boys are never shunned or shamed by sharing the details of the intimate encounter. As a matter of fact, other girls are intrigued by the story and details and will have sex with him even though they know the risk of her reputation. The worst possible idea. And activity. No sex.

No drugs. Being in an altered mental state affects your ability to learn and retain information. Is this a good idea? Why drugs? Why are you seeking an altered mental state? What pain is so intense that drugs is your chosen escape path? What happens if you become addicted? What is the plan for you to recover from that addiction? Who pays for that? What do you miss while you are high and while you are in recovery?

No drugs.

There was a student who came to school after a dosage of 'handlebars.' She was in and altered state for about three hours before she was assessed for drug use. The student had to deal with three immediate issues once the campus police became involved. First, she was sent to the alternative school for 30 days. Secondly, she had to call her mother who was working as a babysitter. The mom had to bring the children with her. The most important part of this was that her mother was an illegal immigrant, which could have led to her deportation. Further, the child could have been put in foster care because that is defined as child endangerment. Finally, the teacher who had to report her state asked the girl how she obtained the drugs. The girl said the guy gave it her for free. The teacher became terrified. She is thinking that all future roads lead to disaster. The thought crossed her mind: 'What was his intention when he gave her that? What will happen next time?'

When the teacher posed these questions, the girl looked afraid, because she had not considered these scenarios and had not thought of the consequences. What if she was forced to sell and distribute drugs as payment for the first amount? What if she was forced to have sex for that as well? What would she do in these scenarios?

Be clear that she was not strong enough to say no in the first place, so what is the likelihood that she will say no to the other scenarios. The dealer picked her because he had been watching her and used her body language to determine that she was a great candidate for his business. He took advantage of her low self-esteem and low self-image. He had asked around the complex to become familiar with her situation. He knew that she made a great target. She had enough pain to make introducing drugs really easy.

No drugs.

No drinking. An alternate state which is designed to distance you from your reality. Imagine being drunk and waking up next to a stranger. What if you wake-up from being drunk, next to a stranger and you are naked? At this point, you do not know if you have had sex; if that sex was protected or not. You do not know what else happened in the process. What if you become pregnant? Alcohol can also be addictive. Again, what will you do to recover from that addiction? What will effected by that addiction: career, education, family relationships? Alcohol has the ability to cause you to speak more frequently, and share some inappropriate information and hurt some feelings. Being drunk could lead to death: yours from alcohol poisoning or car crash and someone else because you hit them.

No drinking.

No cheating. Study! 'But it is hard.' Ask for help. Google. YouTube. Go to tutorials. Ask your parents for a tutor. Find a homework hotline. Do something for your education. It is for your future. School is an integral part of your work ethic. Your work ethic carries you very far and into all parts of your life. The standards you set for yourself and what you achieve is the bar you set for your children. Are you doing as well as your parent(s) did in school? Better than? Not as good as? You compare your grades and your future goals and aspirations to your parent's and other family members.

It is okay to be smart! It is okay to exert yourself on your studies. You had to consider what you need to know to be successful in college and in life.

No cheating!

Reputation matters. Protect it and honor it. Your great reputation elevates not just you, but all who are associated with you. Your poor reputation brings the family down. Your decisions don't only affect you but also others around you.

Because of Jesus, you will experience some trouble, and some persecution. You will be mistreated. You will be questioned. You will be accused. You will be challenged. You will be tested. You will be treated poorly and without dignity. You will be criticized. You will be tempted. You will be tried. You will be angry. You will be tired. You will be disbelieved. You will be fearful. The people who should have helped Jesus treated Him poorly and did not understand His message and lied on Him and caused Him pain. They told Him that He was wrong for performing miracles and healing people, challenged His teachings, tempted Him, and tried to derail His ministry. Jesus lived 33 years without sin. Then He died to save us all. Everyone. Including those who persecuted Him.

Could you do it? Probably not. John 15:18-19 states that they hate you because of Jesus but He did not hate them in return. Jesus saved in spite of His ability to leave them behind.

So when you want to question God about why, then remember that Jesus survived and was elevated. They have tested and tried all of their antics on Jesus, so you are not exempt. Get prepared. Be ready. It will happen to you.

Selfies, Photos, Social Media

You are glamorous! You look AMAZING! You are the bomb! OMG! You are so pretty! Do you know that? Have you heard those compliments? Do you think that about yourself? I hope so and you should.

In those selfies that you share on social media, please make sure that everyone can view those photos. Further, please be sure that the selfie/photo could rest on your pastor's or boss' desk.

Selfies taken in the bathroom in your underwear are not to be taken and certainly not shared on social media. Bathroom selfies become cumbersome to your future college admittance and potential employers and career choices.

Dateline featured a girl who sent some bathroom selfies with underwear and some without clothes. Later, her photos were found on a pornographic website. The sixteen-year-old left school to be homeschooled because of the taunting and shame. At the time of the showing on Dateline, she was 20, in college, and still crying about the situation.

This could have been avoided by never taking nor sending the pictures, no matter how tempting it is to send them, no matter how many times he asks. In the long run, it may cost you more than that relationship.

In 1984, some nude of photos were published while Vanessa L. Williams was Miss America, so she had to resign as Miss America. She took those photos because she needed the money, not realizing that she would later regret those moments and that money. She recovered nicely with an acting career and music career. Not everyone can say the same.

No Nude Photos!

Social Media

Keep your business and your locations and your 'foolishness' off of social media. The websites are FOREVER. Even if they are not, please pretend that they are. Inappropriate photos, comments, and behavior can lead to being overlooked for colleges, athletic positions, and careers. In 2017, Harvard rescinded several acceptances to the school. Athletic scouts are checking your social media pages before offering scholarships to athletes. Pictures with you drinking, doing drugs or/and having sex should definitely not ever be taken or recorded. Future politicians have to answer and account for these types of details all of the time. Control your social media posts as if they are going to show up in court or before Congress. If you may have to defend it later, do not do it now.

WEEK TWELVE REFLECTION

1. What was Jesus' reputation? How did you come to that summary?

____

____

____

____

2. What is your reputation? How was your reputation created/defined?

____

____

____

3. Do you need to improve your reputation? How can you improve your reputation? How long do you think it will take to improve it?

____

____

____

4. Are you the young lady your parents want you to be? Are they proud or embarrassed about you? If that needs to be improved, how will you go about doing so?

____

____

5. Who introduced you to Christ?

6. What is your testimony? When did you accept Christ? When were you baptized? Do you share Christ with others? Who do you share your testimony with?

7. Define leadership—your personal definition. What is God's definition of leadership? Give examples of God's definition of leadership.

8. What does your fellowship and leadership look like? Can you improve either or both? How will you do so?

____

____

____

9. What is your definition of image?

____

____

____

10. What is your image of God?

____

____

____

11. What is your definition of Holy?

____

____

____

12. What is your definition of Righteous?

____

____

____

____

13. What is your definition of forgiving/forgiveness?

____

____

____

14. What is your definition of love/loving?

____

____

____

15. What is your definition of grace?

____

____

____

16. What is your definition of money?

____

____

____

____

17. What is your definition of power?

____

____

____

18. What is your definition of wisdom?

____

____

____

19. What is your definition of creativity?

____

____

____

20. What is God's definition of image? What did He mean in Genesis 1:26-27? How close are you to that image—the likeness of God?

____

---

21. Is what you are doing and looking like supportive of God's desire for your image?

22. Is attitude part of that image? Explain.

23. Is God pleased with your look, your attitude, and your overall disposition?

24. Does God care how you look/what you wear? How do you know? What does He care about exactly?

25. Do you have challenges with skirt length? Do you have challenges with shirt/blouse transparency? Do you have challenges with too tight a fit? Do you have challenges with too much cleavage?

26. Why does your skirt have to be that short? Why can't it be long enough to cover your thigh, which leaves something to the imagination?

27. What message does short and sheer send? What if what you meant to be sexy was actually seen as raunchy?

28. Do you change clothes after you leave your parent(s) presence to something you cannot wear in their presence? If so, why? Do you know what people think of your parents because of your attire?

____

____

____

____

29. Does your attire embarrass your family?

____

____

____

____

30. Share your makeup style and philosophy. Is your makeup so heavy that you look like a different person? How does it make you feel when someone does not recognize you because of your lack of makeup?

____

____

____

____

31. Does your hair vary so drastically that people do not recognize you? How does that make you feel?

____

____

____

32. For those who wear weave or wish to, do you NEED weave? What is wrong with the hair that God gave you?

____

33. With the hair, makeup, and clothes, who are trying to impress? What are you trying to feel better about? Why? What is the benefit of impressing them?

____

34. Are you okay with being known for this for the next 25 years? Are you okay with your daughter wearing that when she is a teenager?

____

35. What do people think of you? How do you know?

____

____

____

____

36. What is a good reputation? How would you maintain that good reputation? What does it take to ruin that good reputation?

____

____

____

____

37. How long does it take to recover from something which damaged your reputation? What has to happen for you to recover that reputation?

____

____

____

____

38. What do you say about girls who have sex and the details of their encounters have been shared? What do others say about them? Are you one of those girls that they talk about? How do you feel when you hear about these girls and their activity?

____

____

____

____

39. Why is your reputation important? Why is a good reputation important?

40. Why aren't drugs a good idea? Do you know that if you are an athlete, the team does random drug checks? Why are you seeking an altered mental state? What pain is so intense that drugs are your chosen escape path?

41. What happens when you become addicted? What is the plan for you to recover from that addiction? Who pays for that? What do you miss while you are high and while you are in recovery?

42. What does it take to say no to drugs? Do you know now to report people who offer you drugs?

43. What would influence you to drink? Where would you get alcohol from? What pain would cause you to seek this altered state?

44. What would you do if you were drunk and woke up the next morning, next to a stranger, naked? What would you do? What would you say? How do you find out if you had sex or not? If that sex was protected or not? What if you become pregnant? What if you were infected with a STD?

45. What is the plan to recover if you become addicted to alcohol? Who pays for that? What do you miss while you are drunk and in recovery?

46. What will be affected by that addiction? School? Family? Sports? Job/career?

____

____

____

47. How do your grades compare to your parents? Better than? About the same? Worse than?

____

____

____

48. Is it okay to be smart? Explain. If not, why not?

____

____

____

49. What can you do to avoid naked and barely clothed selfies? What would happen if a naked photo surfaced of you?

____

____

____

50. What would you do if your social media posts kept you off the sports team of your choice or kept you out of the college of your choice?

____

____

____

____

51. List 5 actions you can do to follow God and Jesus more closely.

____

____

____

____

____

52. What does following Jesus cost you?

____

____

____

____

WEEK TWELVE PROJECT

1. Consider your image. Create a collage of who you are. Include who you want to be.

2. Look at yourself in the mirror for five minutes without criticizing yourself or thinking about what you need to do to improve your looks. Appreciate the work that God did in you. How did you feel after the five minutes?

____

____

____

____

3. Write an affirmation about yourself using the following scriptures: Psalm 139, Deuteronomy 6:5, Psalm 46:1, 10, 1 John 4:19-21, Romans 8:28-39, and Ephesians 3:14-21.

____

____

____

____

____

____

____

____

____

____

WEEK TWELVE JOURNAL

WEEK THIRTEEN

Parents

[26] and she said to him, "Pardon me, my lord. As surely as you live, I am the woman who stood here beside you praying to the LORD. [27] I prayed for this child, and the LORD has granted me what I asked of him.

1 Samuel 1:26-27

[13] Then people brought little children to Jesus for him to place his hands on them and pray for them. But the disciples rebuked them.
[14] Jesus said, "Let the little children come to me, and do not hinder them, for the kingdom of heaven belongs to such as these."

Matthew 19:13-14

[20] Children, obey your parents in everything, for this pleases the Lord. [21] Fathers, do not embitter your children, or they will become discouraged.

Colossians 3:20-21

2 Samuel 2:15-25	Malachi 4:6
Deuteronomy 4:9	Ephesians 6:1-3
Joel 1:31	Joshua 24:17
Proverbs 23:13	Psalm 22:9
Proverbs 31:28	Proverbs 17:25
Exodus 20:12	Psalm 112:2
Proverbs 23:22	Proverbs 29:17
Hebrews 12:7	Proverbs 17:21
Leviticus 19:3	1 Samuel 2:19
Proverbs 19:18	Proverbs 20:20

Proverbs 13:24   Proverbs 29:15

Genesis 18:19

The definition of love should start with your parents. Unfortunately, that is not the case for some. By God's design, they love you just because they actually birthed you. Some of you are an extraordinary miracle because you were not actually supposed to be here according to the story that you were told. So if you were taught love by your parents and you are loved by your parents, then you should be able to love others and love yourself.

Parents may seem difficult at times. Consider the job description of a parent.

Want Ad:

Needed: Parents for this future ___________________ (doctor, gymnast, lawyer, teacher, etc.) with a difficult spirit, who wants to love selectively, and has a moody disposition after the age of 14. She will be a sweet daughter until age 13, then something will change. She may lie or steal, cheat or deceive. She may be a successful student or she may have a learning disability. Regardless of how she behaves, you will be required to feed, clothe, and provide her shelter. Parents, you are selected for this unknown bundle of joy, which may excite or disappoint, love or hate, succeed or fail, learn or reject. Whatever happens, you are her steward and I expect you to parent full-time and as creatively as legally as possible. Thank you, potential parent for your acceptance of this thankless and rewarding assignment and experience.

Sincerely,

God.

Understand that you did not choose your parent but your parents did not choose you either. You were assigned to one another by God—the Creator of everyone.

So first off, let's establish respect for the parents. Respect them full-time. Listen. Obey. Learn. Your entire life is the report card of your parents—whether they actually contribute to your life's success or not.

Consider how you discard people who disrespect you because of some simple words, yet you don't wash dishes, do not do your homework, nor clean your room, nor clean your bathroom, and do not keep your life together.

Why don't they discard you? Because they do not want to. They are also responsible for what you know and they are responsible for what you do not know. Act and obey like you understand that.

This relationship has to last for the rest of your lives. You need them and they need you. So how do you make this work? Let's go to work.

Parenting is a hard job. You feel that being a child is a hard job. Parents will disagree and will always win the argument. They pay the bills, arrange your education and your extra-curricular activities. They sacrifice what they would buy for themselves for you to have what you need. You do not recognize it or know about it but it's real.

God expects you to be certain type of child: respect your parents, love your parents, obey your parents, exceed your parents academically and professionally, and finally, you are to represent them well at all times.

Respect

Respect your parents at all times. Even when you don't feel that they deserve it. There are only a few events, activities, or situations where your lack of respect can be understood. Baring those details, respect is required. God refers to respect as honor. No talking back. Listening and obeying. Learn to communicate with respect. Girls are known for tone that seems disrespectful. Learn to communicate without having an attitude and a disrespectful tone. This means that you listen completely. Then you **don't** smack your teeth, roll your eyes, mumble under your breath, speak disrespectfully, or ignore your parent. Communication is best learned with your parent. You will learn what the world expects regarding communication with your parents.

Your parent's job is to teach you so it is best that you learn. Stop with the wall of defense when your parent is speaking with you. You need to demonstrate body language which says that you are listening and you are hearing what your parent is saying to you. Body language is also a part of communication.

So tone, body language, and the actual words are the components of communication. The intention of those words can be considered as well. What you say and how you say it are equally important. So listen to yourself when you speak. How do you sound? Would you listen to yourself when you speak? How does how you sound make you feel? How does how you sound make others feel?

Do you leave others with their dignity when you speak to them? Or do they wither internally after you all part ways?

Communication drives the world and all that happens with it. What kind of communicator are you going to be? How will others perceive your communication? How will they respond to you? Will you be the person everyone flocks to or everyone flees from?

Love

They should be loved. They are your parents. Love them unconditionally; not based on what you have or don't; what they can buy or not. Your parents are judged on your character, not your possessions. How you achieve and maintain those possessions are how you are 'judged.'

What makes you love them or not? What makes your love conditional?

Thankful, Grateful and Appreciative

Are you thankful for having parents? Do you know what your life would be like if your parents were not raising you? What if you were being raised by foster parent(s) or in a group home? What if your parents were both dead or incarcerated or some combination of the two?

Parents want appreciative children. You were taught to say thank you. You were taught to be grateful. Are you? Does your parent agree? Appreciation also is in deed—behavior. When your parents buy items, they put a mental replacement date on it. For example, tennis shoes should last about a year or two if you just wear them to school. That is the time for a child whose foot has stopped growing. If you play a sport, that time shortens from six months to a year. So when you leave the shoes outside in the rain or the mud and the shoes are three (3) months old, you are unappreciative.

Consider what your parent could do for herself with the money they spend on you. When was the last time your parent did something for him or herself? What do they want to do with some extra money that they would have spent on you?

Appreciation goes a long way.

Parents are also supposed to be teachers and leaders. They are to show you what the Lord says and what both of you are supposed to do.

Parents are not perfect, but you already know that. However, they are to also be forgiven for the their mistakes and sins.

Parents need to be able to trust you with everything. Money. Time. Resources. Driving. School. Sports. Life.

Consider this situation: You were supposed to be on a freeway on the north side of town, but you decided to go somewhere else without your parents knowledge or consent. You were on the south freeway instead. There was an accident which was later labeled fatal, meaning that someone died. Your parents hear the news and dismiss the information because you were not in that area—or so they thought. But now because of the traffic you will be late getting home. What if that had been you dead on the freeway?

Let's look at the other scenario: you were actually involved in the accident but didn't die. You are alive to tell your parents that you were in the accident, but they need to come get you at the hospital where you were taken for observation. They drop the bombshell: the other person in the accident died, which could have been you. As this information sinks in and the reality of the situation and its severity washed over your parents, they start reacting in a variety of ways; none of which you can anticipate but one thing is certain: their trust for you is gone.

Was your adventure worth the total outcome? And no, you never thought of any of those details or outcomes.

Trust cannot easily be restored, so it should be fervently protected. This is your biggest challenge: being trusted.

The Roles

Parent	You
Love	love
Provide	listen
Protector	obey
Teacher	learn
Nurturer	be trustworthy

This is a non-comprehensive answer and the answers go on and on. Parenting is a non-prescriptive job which means they have to respond to unforeseen situations and circumstances. Parenting is an on call job, one never knowing that the other end of the phone holds, the message in that email, the knock at the door, or the words that come out of your mouth.

It is the scariest feat ever attempted by anyone.

Keeping you alive, feeding you, bathing you without drowning you, nurturing you to the best possible person in spite of the world's intentions and beliefs, and teaching you enough character so that you can be a productive citizen. So when she asks you to study, she's helping to build your work ethic and to develop healthy habits for a productive life.

What do you think that your parent should expect of you? Why don't you think that those expectations are unreasonable? Why do you act like your parents are doing something that they do not have the right to do when they discipline you? Teach you? Talk to you? Pray for you?

Parents are graded and labeled based on what you do, regardless of what they tried to do to equip you to do. In the world, people will ask you 'didn't your mother teach you anything?' when you are doing something contrary to the teaching which is appropriate at that time. You will be challenged about the teachings of your parents when you cross societal boundaries regarding behavior. The exact words are: "she does not have any home training."

Proud

Strive to make sure that your parent(s) can be proud of you. Good grades. Good behavior. Trustworthy. Honest. Completing the societal measures of achievement based on education and career. Obviously, avoid jail time and other issues which cause your life to have obstacles.

Take time to be sure that even if your parents are not people you can be proud of, change your situation so that your children will be proud of you.

Parenting is a hard, thankless job and still people want to do it. Some people feel that parenting is validation of who they are. Parenting is work—make it joyful for your parents. Parents do not get to take vacation, or sick days or time off or a break. Every day, all day, they are on call, and when the phone rings, there is a chance that there is something wrong with their child.

David sinned with Bathsheba (2 Samuel 12:15-25) and made it worse by trying to cover it up and caused a man, Bathsheba's husband, to be killed. Yes, there was infidelity in the Bible. The child, that was born to those parents as the outcome of that sin, died. God took that child.

Before God took that child, David fasted and prayed for the seven days until the baby's death. The dad did not eat for seven days. He stopped working. He slept on the ground in a sackcloth while he asked the Lord to heal the child. Instead of healing the baby, God took the baby. When David found out, he bathed, dressed and went to worship God.

That is what parents to for our children. God calls parents to sacrifice. To fast. To pray.

Have you ever heard your parents pray? Do you think that their prayer is corny or unnecessary? Do you know that your parents are charged with prayer for your life?

In 1 Samuel 1:27-28, Hannah prayed for her son that she initially thought she would never see. She prayed for this child and then gave that son to the Lord as she promised that she would when she asked for a child.

How would your life look differently if your parents did not pray for you? Would life look differently if you submitted to your parent's prayers? Do you know that you learn to pray by listening to those who pray? What does God want you to learn by listening to your parent's prayers? What will you do when you are in a time of need if you didn't learn to pray?

In Matthew 19:13-14, Jesus speaks to His disciples about children. Jesus requests them to be brought to Him. Don't view that request as an optional assignment. Parents are to bring their children to Jesus. Please understand that God has sent for you and He will get you back to Him. By whatever means He chooses.

In Deuteronomy 4:9, the Lord demands that parents teach their children what they know to all living generations. God charges us to teach, so when you do not know something, your parent is accountable and responsible. Learn. Let your parent do her job.

Colossians 3:20-21 commands that children obey their parents because this pleases the Lord. The next command is that fathers are not to embitter their children. Translation: do not aggravate your children because you will discourage them. Not to aggravate does not mean not to discipline or correct. Do not aggravate means love when they discipline you, teach you with integrity and without judgement or sarcasm, and lead by example, denying themselves the desires of the flesh.

Malachi 4:6 commands that God will turn the hearts of parents and children toward each other. You need the heart of your parent. Your parent needs your heart. You need each other's hearts. Your heart is motivation to your parents. Your parents' heart is motivation to you. The heart is an investment of the emotional resources you have, which is how you show you love people and are concerned about people. Both you and your parent need the heart of the other, so that you can remain encouraged to keep the relationship healthy.

Daughters, you need your parents. You may become discouraged about your overall situation. You need to consider the value of that person, as they are valuable in their jobs, with their friends, and within their social circles. You know of girls without parents. You do not envy those girls, rather they envy you. Do not take your parents for granted.

WEEK THIRTEEN REFLECTION

1. What are the expectations of your parents?

____

____

____

____

2. What do your parents expect of you? Why don't you think that those expectations are unreasonable?

____

____

____

____

3. Define love. List examples of how you demonstrate your love for your parents. List examples of how your parents demonstrate love towards you.

____

____

____

____

4. Define respect. When do you respect your parents? When do you disrespect your parents? Why?

____

____

____

____

5. Why do you have trouble listening to your parents? How do you speak to others? How do you sound to others when you speak? Would you listen to yourself when you speak? How does how you sound make you feel?

____

____

____

____

6. Do you leave others with their dignity when you speak to them? Or do they wither internally after you all part ways?

____

____

____

____

7. What kind of communicator are you going to be? How will others perceive your communication? How would you respond to you? Will you be the person everyone flocks to or flees from?

____

____

____

8. What makes you love them or not? What makes your love conditional? When is your love unconditional?

____

____

____

____

9. Are you thankful for having parents? Do you know other children who do not have parents? What would your life look like if you did not have parents? Or if you were not raised by your biological parents? What if you were raised by foster parents or in a group home? What if one of your parents were incarcerated or dead or both?

____

____

____

____

10. Are you grateful? Do your parents agree?

____

____

____

____

11. When was the last time your parent did something for him or herself? What do they want to do with some extra money that they would have spent on you?

____

____

____

____

12. Define trust. What does it take to gain trust? What does it take to lose trust?

____

____

____

____

13. Why do you act like your parents are doing something that they do not have the right to do when they discipline you? Teach you? Talk to you? Pray for you?

____

____

____

____

14. Define proud. Are you proud of yourself? Are your parents proud of you? Are you proud of them? What would it take for you to be proud of yourself? What would it take for you to be proud of your parents? What would it take for your parents to be proud of you?

____

____

____

____

15. Do you pray? Do you ever see or hear your parent(s) pray? What would your life be like if they did not pray for you? If they did not teach you, how would you learn to pray? What would you do in your time of need if you did not know how to pray?

____

____

____

____

16. Define fasting. Do your parents fast? Do you fast? What could you fast from other than food?

____

____

____

____

17. What would your parents teach you? Should your parents let the internet and school teach you everything? Summarize Deuteronomy 4:9 based on your life.

____

____

____

____

18. Define obedience. Are you obedient? Why not? Reflect on Colossians 3:20-21. How can you arrange your life so that you can be obedient?

____

____

____

____

19. Summarize Malachi 4:6. How can you be closer to your parents? How can your parents be closer to you?

____

____

____

____

WEEK THIRTEEN PROJECTS

1. Write a parental job description.

____

____

____

____

____

2. Write your job description.

____

____

____

____

____

3. Create a job chart/calendar with household duties, homework assignments, and extracurricular schedule.

4. Ask your mother for her calendar and see what her schedule looks like before she gets home.

WEEK THIRTEEN JOURNAL

WEEK FOURTEEN

Ruth: Persist through what is right

[4] At this they wept aloud again. Then Orpah kissed her mother-in-law goodbye, but Ruth clung to her. [15] "Look," said Naomi, "your sister-in-law is going back to her people and her gods. Go back with her." [16] But Ruth replied, "Don't urge me to leave you or to turn back from you. Where you go I will go, and where you stay I will stay. Your people will be my people and your God my God. [17] Where you die I will die, and there I will be buried. May the LORD deal with me, be it ever so severely, if even death separates you and me." [18] When Naomi realized that Ruth was determined to go with her, she stopped urging her.

Ruth 1:4, 15-18

As you grow up you will find out how you define family. Observe your family on a daily basis, on holidays, and weekends. What is a matriarch? Who is the matriarch in your family? What is a patriarch? Who is the patriarch in your family?

Family defines you. What does your family do that is unique amongst your family? What does family mean to you? What do you do as a family that you like the most?

Every culture has a different definition of family. You can define it however you want. You need to be able to define it, help to develop it, and to defend it, if necessary.

All of us have taken note of what happens at home and compared the notes between friends. Does that comparison make you more grateful? It should make you more grateful for what you experience as a family. Based on what you see, how do you contribute to the family experience? As you consider family, who is included? Define friends. Are friends ever considered family? Are family considered friends?

In these scriptures, Naomi is Ruth's mother-in-law. Ruth was married to Naomi's son until he died. At the point of the husband and son's death, Naomi wanted to go back to her homeland, so Ruth followed. When Naomi told Ruth to return to her own homeland, Ruth rejected that idea with zeal, Ruth 1:15-18.

Families take a stand for each other. Families stay together and they grow strong together. Families are designed to move together strategically to achieve some overall family goals. Do you know what you family's goal is? How do you contribute to that goal? How could your activity/behavior still that goal?

Families keep their disagreements internal and they solve their issues and do not let issues fester.

Families have a legacy and a purpose. What is your family's legacy? What is your family's purpose? How do you know? How did you find out? Who told you the legacy? Who shared the family purpose? Family is forever. Family is not to be traded. Family is not to be sacrificed.

Family is a place to belong. Family defines all places where you want to belong. From school to social settings to career choices, the way your family is defined defines your life in many aspects.

God created family which started with two people, those people started the world. How do you participate in keeping the family together? How do you uphold God's definition of family that God designed?

Friends are hard to come by, friends that you keep for a lifetime, to whom you can be loyal, and with whom you can share the details of your life. Friends also keep you accountable for doing what is right. At all times. Friends should also help each other to elevate their lives to the next level.

Friends keep each other out of trouble. Likewise, friends also help each other through pain and disappointment. Friends help you refine your style, possibly add some polish and finesse. Family develops your value system. Friends test those values.

WEEK FOURTEEN REFLECTION

1. Define family. Who are your immediate family members?

____

____

____

____

2. Who is your favorite family member? Why?

____

____

____

3. What traditions does your family employ? Why those particular traditions? How long has that been a tradition? How do you contribute to that tradition?

____

____

____

____

4. What are the legacies of your family? What are you known for, for example, education, etc.? How do you fit into that legacy? What will you contribute to that legacy?

____

____

____

____

5. Based on what your family is, what will you do differently when you start your own branch of the family?

____

____

____

____

6. What do you want to change about your family?

____

____

____

____

7. What makes you proud to be in that family? What embarrasses you about your family?

____

____

____

____

8. What makes your family proud about you? What makes your family embarrassed about you?

____

____

____

____

9. What do you want to understand better about your family? Who is going to explain/share that information with you?

____

____

____

____

10. Are there any family secrets that you have discovered? How are you handling that?

____

____

____

____

11. Do you value family? On a scale of 1—10, how much? Why this number? What could increase that number? Have you shared that? What would devalue that number?

____

____

____

____

12. Describe your ideal family. How close is yours to your description?

____

____

____

____

13. What did you think of Ruth and her loyalty to Naomi? What did you learn from that situation?

____

____

____

14. Look up the word mantra. What is your family's mantra? If you don't have one, then create one.

____

____

____

WEEK FOURTEEN PROJECT

1. Create a family tree.

2. Plan a family dinner that occurs monthly. Put together some family rules (no cell phones at dinner, etc.) for this dinner and designated other family time. Bring a discussion topic each month.

____

____

____

____

____

____

3. Plan a yearly family vacation.

____

____

____

____

____

____

WEEK FOURTEEN JOURNAL

WEEK FIFTEEN

Grace and Mercy Defined

[1] Answer me when I call to you, my righteous God. Give me relief from my distress; have mercy on me and hear my prayer.

Psalm 4:1

[1] Therefore, I urge you, brothers and sisters, in view of God's mercy, to offer your bodies as a living sacrifice, holy and pleasing to God—this is your true and proper worship.

Romans 12:1

[14] David said to Gad, "I am in deep distress. Let us fall into the hands of the LORD, for his mercy is great; but do not let me fall into human hands."

2 Samuel 24:14

[15] Here is a trustworthy saying that deserves full acceptance: Christ Jesus came into the world to save sinners—of whom I am the worst. [16] But for that very reason I was shown mercy so that in me, the worst of sinners, Christ Jesus might display his immense patience as an example for those who would believe in him and receive eternal life.

1 Timothy 1:15-16

Daniel 9:18	1 Peter 2:10
Luke 1:50	Psalm 51:1
Psalm 9:13	Psalm 69:16
Nehemiah 9:31	Psalm 79:8
Psalm 86:16	Romans 11:30
1 Timothy 1:2	

Grace is defined as the freely given, unmerited favor and love of God. Grace is also the influence of spirit of God operating in humans to regenerate or strengthen them.

Mercy is defined as something that gives evidence of divine favor. Mercy is also defined as compassionate or kindly forbearance shown toward and offender, an enemy, or other person in one's power; compassion, pity, or benevolence.

2 Samuel 24:14

David has called out to God in deep distress and all that he asked was for mercy. David asks that only the Lord judge and punish. Mercy is being forgiven without consequence or very minimal consequence.

David prayed then offered a sacrifice. After three years of famine, God ended the famine because of David's confession and sacrifice. What will God do when you tell the truth and make good on your situation through confession? How do your sins cost your family and friends, and people that you don't know?

Romans 12:1-2

Paul teaches us that God has already been merciful but he does not give details about God's merciful acts but based on the definition, you should have some personal details.

When you consider David's actions and Paul's teachings, your mercy will come through your personal sacrifice of yourself. The personal sacrifice means that deny your desires to sin such as lies, deceit, laziness, sex, gossip, overeating, and other sins which cause you to be separated from God. Paul teaches us to renew our minds to Jesus and God—will God approve your thoughts and actions?

What can you sacrifice to give God so that He is glorified? What can you sacrifice to show God your commitment to Him?

1 Timothy 1:15-16

Because you are shown mercy, then you are not to be judged. You too are to show mercy. Mercy is supposed to be transferable. It is what you pass on to people you meet who are broken. Jesus has been patient with you. You then should be able to be patient with others. This is hard, especially then someone has wronged you. It is our charge from Jesus to show mercy to others because of what God does for us, especially without our knowledge.

Psalm 4:1

"Thank you for the power and the privilege of prayer." Prayer is the encouraged conversation with God where He speaks to you and you speak to Him. During this time of prayer, you are completely transparent with God and because of the power of the Holy Spirit, your true self will be revealed, especially to yourself. Prayer is the place where you share your petitions, intentions, and thoughts. Just because God hears your prayer, does not mean that He answers immediately. Hearing you does not mean that you will get exactly what you desire, or at least not the way you wanted it.

When Hannah asked for a child, she was given a son; not in her time, but in God's time.

Prayer requires patience as well as understanding that God may answer you in a different way than you want. So wait on God and anticipate God-style awesome.

Some of your needs drive you to prayer. This prayer does not mean that your request is bad if you do not receive what you request. It just means that your request is not in the will of God at that time, for this occasion.

Grace and mercy defined means that you will consider that God rescues more often than you realize. You cheated on that test, but didn't get caught. Because you didn't get caught, you stopped cheating because you realized that the consequences were worse than the possible grade, because you didn't study. You had sex but didn't get caught, or didn't get pregnant or didn't ruin your reputation or didn't contract a sexually transmitted disease.

Grace and mercy offers you an opportunity to reflect, repent and reconcile on your situation and make a different future decision. It is your DO-OVER where you get another chance to do it God's way.

Grace and mercy are not infinite and should be used wisely when gifted.

We don't deserve everything we get and we don't get everything we deserve.

Mercy and Grace!

WEEK FIFTEEN REFLECTION

1. When have you experienced God's grace and mercy? Be specific.

____

____

____

____

2. How will you explain God's grace and mercy to others? How will you help them to recognize it?

____

____

____

____

3. When have you ignored God's grace and mercy, and still followed the wrong path?

____

____

____

____

4. Who has experienced grace and mercy that you have witnessed?

____

____

____

____

5.   Who inspired you to be better as a Christian?

____

____

____

____

6.   How will you better recognize God's grace and mercy going forward?

____

____

____

____

WEEK FIFTEEN PROJECT

1. List the sins that you need help avoiding and then list the 'obstacles' which prevent that sin from being easy to commit.

____

____

____

____

____

____

2. Post the scriptures listed at the beginning of the chapter where you can see them daily.

WEEK FIFTEEN JOURNAL

WEEK SIXTEEN

Eve: To Whom Much is Required

[22] Then the LORD God made a woman from the rib he had taken out of the man, and he brought her to the man.
[23] The man said, "This is now bone of my bones and flesh of my flesh; she shall be called 'woman,' for she was taken out of man."
[24] That is why a man leaves his father and mother and is united to his wife, and they become one flesh.
[25] Adam and his wife were both naked, and they felt no shame.

Genesis 2:22-25

Imagine if you were the first woman, the only woman—the woman God made from the rib of the man which God made from dust of the Earth. God chose Eve. The best news is that God chose you as well.

God planned something for the world that changed because Eve sinned and convinced Adam to do the same. The weight of the world rested upon the shoulders of those two. They changed the course of the world in one afternoon, in one act.

Luke 12:48 KJV reads, 'To whom much is given, much is required.'

God has some expectations of you. What are those expectations? What are those attached requirements? Eve was supposed to follow directions, but she violated the rules and was disobedient. You are expected to be special. You are elite. You are expected to reach certain levels in your life.

Why are the expectations so high? Your parents and family have a legacy and standards. You should be prepared to meet those standards. Why do you have a mental block against their expectations? You are expected to make good grades. Good grades are defined as 80's and 90's or A's and B's. There is no excuse for anything less. What else are you going to do other than make good grades?

You are expected to have great behavior. Great behavior means obedience at home and at school and in public. It also means respecting adults, arriving to class on time, turning in all of your assignments, and being able to communicate effectively. This is a practiced and learned situation in some cases. Overall, however, the biggest responsibility is not to embarrass your family with illegal behavior, such as drugs, alcohol and theft, or other crimes.

Every family has a legacy whether good, bad or indifferent. You are expected to contribute to that legacy and make it better. So if college is the expectation, then that is the expectation and it is non-negotiable. The degree is just a tool. There is a classic adage that says, 'I would rather have it and not need it, than to need it and not have it.' What that means is that you decided not to go to college for all of the excuses: that's too much work, I don't want to do all of that work, I want to escape my parents hand of authority. That is fine until you are 27 years old (or any age), and you apply for a job which requires a degree, the degree you rejected because you were tired of school or that your parents would "control" you a little longer, and you are "great for the position but unfortunately, because you don't have a degree, you are not qualified for the position." How does that sound? How does that make you feel? What would you do if that were your situation? Consider that very carefully when you consider dropping out of college, or not going at all.

Great behavior includes dress code. If you have to change clothes when you arrive somewhere or change clothes before you arrive home, then that outfit is inappropriate! What are you going to do when you are caught with that outfit on and you embarrass your parents? What happens when you are not selected for something you really wanted to be a part of but your attire/clothing caused them to say no?

Then there is social media. The pictures you share and the posts you make are representative of your character. When you post underwear selfies, and nude photos and posts which are designed to bully, you are not attractive to colleges and careers. This is not the legacy of the family. Social media can ruin your chances for many opportunities. College athletes are being screened through social media. Coaches and recruiters are avoiding players with horrible social media presence.

Employers are watching social media pages of employees and potential employees and they will take disciplinary action(s) as necessary, up to and including termination. Your social media can undermine the image of the organization. Since this impacts them financially and holistically, you may be fired. All because of a misplaced social media post. Not a good choice.

"To whom much is given, much is required." Luke 12:48. You ask for a lot but want to do very little. Respect. Grades. Culture. Behavior. Clean room. Education. Life plan. Career. Independence. You cannot dismiss your responsibilities or shirk your expectations. Your parents do much. Your parent(s) sacrifice for you. They sometimes buy items which they cannot afford to satisfy you. They sometimes don't buy something for themselves because they buy something for you. You ask for things, even if they are absolutely necessary when they are not convenient for the budget.

However, you still eat in your room and leave that trash in your room at the risk of bugs and stench. You will not clean your room. You have clothes everywhere, on the floor, and all over your bed. When your mother asks you to clean up or come here, you roll your eyes. You bring home less than admirable grades and use excuses to make sure that you feel justified in those low grades.

You won't wash the dishes. Or clean the kitchen. You don't cook.

Because of the family legacy, you are expected to do all that is asked of you. Period.

Stop making faces, having an attitude, making excuses, and avoiding the expectations.

Eve's disobedience costs her. Eve's disobedience costs you. What does your disobedience cost you? The family? The future generations?

WEEK SIXTEEN REFLECTION

1. Who is Eve? What was expected of Eve?

____

____

____

____

2. What did Eve do wrong?

____

____

____

____

3. What was the consequence to her disobedience?

____

____

____

____

4. What is expected of you? What do your parents want for you? Why are you trying to avoid those expectations?

____

____

____

____

5. Why do you think that they are expecting too much?

____

____

____

____

6. Based on your own desires, what do you expect of yourself? How do you share those expectations with others?

____

____

____

____

7. How did you develop those self-expectations? How different are they from what your parent(s)/family expects?

____

____

____

____

8. What do your friends think of your expectations and your parent's expectations?

____

---

9. What will the world expect of you? Will you be ready to meet those expectations?

---

10. What are your daily requirements? What are your future requirements?

WEEK SIXTEEN PROJECTS

1. Have a family meeting where you will agree on the expectations and requirements and write them out and will contract with you so that we can be successful as a family.

____

____

____

____

____

____

____

____

____

____

2. Add to your vision board.

WEEK SIXTEEN JOURNAL

WEEK SEVENTEEN

Martha: A Bad Attitude and Wrong Motives

[40] But Martha was distracted by all the preparations that had to be made. She came to him and asked, "Lord, don't you care that my sister has left me to do the work by myself? Tell her to help me!"
[41] "Martha, Martha," the Lord answered, "you are worried and upset about many things, [42] but few things are needed—or indeed only one. Mary has chosen what is better, and it will not be taken away from her."

Luke 10:40-42 (NIV)

Every time Martha opens her mouth, we are afraid. She does not think about the implications of her words. Or her tone. Or her posture. Or her disposition.

Martha is so outrageously bold that she blames Jesus for Lazarus' death (John 11:20-24, 39) and then goes on to argue with Jesus about His abilities. While in conversation with Jesus, Martha misses the very message that Jesus teaches. She totally misunderstands the importance of His presence. She did not understand the death of Lazarus was designed to show that God can do what He pleases whenever He chooses.

Martha tattled on Mary for not helping in the kitchen (Luke 10:38-41) and was frustrated and upset. Jesus told Martha that she was worried about the wrong thing. Mary had her priorities correct. Mary knew that Jesus would be leaving soon. For that matter so did Martha but she did not actually VALUE their time the same as Mary did.

Jesus shared directly with Martha what should have been important and what He expected to be priority and she still missed it.

She is not remorseful or reflective either. She does not reflect back on what Jesus said directly to her which should cause her to think I should go back to Jesus and apologize and then talk with Him about what I have learned, mentioning how I might approach this differently in the future.

Martha has a less than appropriate attitude about life in general. Between panic and her argumentative nature and her misplaced priorities, Martha does not seem like a Christian, at least not a mature Christian. Martha does not act like that she has spent any time with Jesus.

Do we know anyone like that—someone who acts like Martha? Do you act like Martha?

Jesus teaches Martha directly—a desire some of us have. Martha did not seem to understand the value of having Jesus present daily.

Martha's poor motives are the second issue she has. Who is she concerned with? SELF! Martha wanted everything her way and as she saw it. She did not think outside of her own bubble, never beyond herself. Does that sound familiar?

Jesus taught Martha, and consequently teaches us to put others before ourselves. Our maturity enables us to consider the whole picture and not the immediate gratification we have previously pursued.

Martha demonstrates the normal tendencies of self but Jesus shows us how to elevate our thinking, compassion and service to include others (everyone) and get past ourselves. Jesus demonstrates that if we take care of God's business then God will take care of us.

Martha does not think about the bigger picture. Jesus has already told everyone that His days were numbered. Literally. The way John recounts the account, just after the meal at Martha's house, it would be five days until Jesus is crucified. When you consider all that people want to know about Jesus and from Jesus and to know Martha used her time unwisely makes us look at time differently.

Martha blamed, argued, and tattled. Instead, what could she have been doing with such precious time?

WEEK SEVENTEEN REFLECTION

1. Who is Martha to Jesus? Why does she have so much access to Jesus?

____

____

____

2. Why does Martha think that Jesus is late? If you had to grade Marth's faith, what would her grade be? Based on that grading system, how would you grade yourself?

____

____

____

3. What is your opinion of Martha? Do you relate to her or do you relate to Mary? Explain.

____

____

____

4. What would you have done when Jesus met you about the death of Lazarus? What were you expecting of Jesus? Did you understand Jesus' lesson to Martha? What was the lesson? Is there anywhere in your life that you can apply that lesson(s)?

____

5. Why was Martha so bold in her behavior and words with Jesus? Do you think that Martha should have chosen her words more carefully? Can you recall a time when you should have been quiet rather than speaking?

6. Do you listen to God as you should? Do you blame Jesus for your situation or your unfortunate circumstances?

7. What should Martha have said when Jesus arrived? What should Martha have said when Jesus wept?

8. What did the "late" resurrection of Lazarus teach you?

____

____

____

____

9. Do you consider the lessons Jesus is teaching when you have unfavorable situations? Explain.

____

____

____

____

10. What do you wish you could talk personally to Jesus about right now?

____

____

____

____

11. How do you think Martha felt when Jesus was crucified? Do you think she reflected back to those occasions? Do you think that she regretted the way she spent their time together? Do you think she wished that she could have that time back?

____

____

____

---

12. Do you think that Martha was selfish? Why was Martha selfish? Are you selfish? Why? Who do you know that is not selfish?

13. Do you question God? Not ask God questions, but do you question God?

14. After God shared with Martha that Mary was doing the right thing and that her motives were pure, what did Martha do (using your understanding of the text) and what should she be doing? What would you have done?

15. What can we do so that God is first, others are served, and our motives are pure?

WEEK SEVENTEEN PROJECT

1. Write a letter to someone apologizing for being selfish.

2. List how you can spend your time better.

____

____

____

____

3. Write a letter to God about questions and concerns you have.

____

____

____

____

____

____

____

____

____

____

____

WEEK SEVENTEEN JOURNAL

WEEK EIGHTEEN

Naomi: Transparency and Direction

Ruth 1-4

Naomi was widowed and alone. Her husband and sons were dead. The sons left two daughters-in-law, who stayed with Naomi. Because of the laws at that time, Naomi had no job and no husband and no life. She wanted to die. She could only marry to certain people as well.

Right when Naomi wanted to quit, God helped Ruth to speak up. Ruth sets Naomi's heart on fire by saying, "Where you go, I'll go." Naomi had to continue being Mom and Mother-in-Law. So they traveled to the hometown of their relatives. Upon their arrival, they settled into everyday life. Then Boaz showed up. Right behavior. Right words. Right motives. Right heart.

Naomi is by definition wise. This wisdom leads to knowledge and wisdom and understanding of God and His plans. Naomi makes the path clear for Ruth, showing her the rules and expectations, traditions, and standards, pitfalls, and special accommodations. Ruth listens with fervor and respect. Ruth takes action accordingly.

Some of you have a mother, grandmother, aunt, and older cousins. Some of us do not have any of those people. But everyone can have a Naomi. Naomi was wise and she unselfishly shared that wisdom. It was helpful that Ruth was cooperative. If your 'Naomi' is not popping into you mind, then consider looking a little more intentionally. Maybe it is someone with the career that you want or in your desired field of educational studies. Maybe she is your mom or another family member.

Naomi offered transparency. She shared details and was honest. This combination is rare. Most people do what they do for selfish gain or self-preservation. The popular phrase is: 'what is in it for me?' Most people don't do anything without there being a reward or benefit, mostly financial. With transparency being rare, you too have to learn to be transparent.

There is immense value in transparency and honesty. Naomi shares that. Ruth respects her for it and the life-long bond is reinforced. Naomi gives direction. That direction is based on wisdom. Naomi used her own experience to give the best of herself to Ruth.

Who does that for you? Are you aware of the sacrifice that is required to do that? Are you cooperative and receptive? Obedient? Compliant? Are you worth helping? Pleasant to help?

WEEK EIGHTEEN REFLECTION

1. Describe Naomi's characteristics. What do you admire about her (5 characteristics)? Why?

____

____

____

____

2. Do you have a mentor? A wise woman in your life in addition to your family?

____

____

____

____

3. Who mentors you? Invests in you? Shares wisdom with you?

____

____

____

____

4. Who knows your dreams? Goals? Aspirations? What are they doing to help you to reach and to achieve those dreams, goals and aspirations?

____

____

---

5. Who gives you direction and advice? Who is ideal to do that?

---

6. Are you aware of the sacrifice required to help you?

---

7. Are you cooperative and compliant? Receptive? Obedient? Pleasant to help?

---

8. Are you worth helping? Why?

____

____

Are there times when you are hard to help? When do you not listen?

____

____

____

____

WEEK EIGHTEEN PROJECTS

1. Write a letter to your mentor, your Naomi. Include what you hope that she can help you to achieve and what you want to learn overall.

2. Make a goal sheet. Include the next 1 year, 3, 5, 10, and 15 year goals.

WEEK EIGHTEEN JOURNAL

WEEK NINETEEN

Esther: Overcoming Your Position

Esther 1-9

Esther! Whew! This story is amazing! There is a song that says, "I started from the bottom, now I am here." Maybe you have heard it? Well if not, let's explore. The song is written by an artist who had nothing and now you are singing this song. You may not know his name but you have sung that song. Or at least heard someone else singing it.

Esther does not know the song but she knows the experience. She was in a group of hundreds of women who were selected to audition to be the next queen of her country—a job that she did not want, but could not be removed from the process. Esther was a teenager. This 'audition' may include sex with the King. If that occurred, she would not be able to return to general society. She would remain as a concubine to the king—not the ideal life; not what girls dream of.

But if she does everything well then she is the next Queen, except for the fact that her family background is a little sordid: the cousin is Jewish. This was not acceptable in that culture. So did she have a chance? She should not have but yet she did.

Well Esther participated in the selection process and asked the right questions, took the correct gift, and was chosen to be queen.

Do you know how great it feels to be chosen? Sure you do. You have been chosen for some activities and events.

The most important choosing was God chose you! God chose you to do and to be and to achieve and to live and to breathe. God chose you. Without God choosing you, you would not be here on Earth for others to reject.

Consider how Esther felt to be chosen. It is more to this life to being chosen though. Now, she has to work to maintain that 'impossible to get,' 'to die for,' and 'a million girls would kill for this job' position. Well, Esther overcame obstacle number one: she became Queen. The second thing was to understand how to assist with peace.

Esther had an awesome opportunity to bring two cultures together. She did that through exposing the harm wanted Hammon to bring to Mordecai. The King listened to Queen Esther and took action against Hammon because of the evidence Esther presented.

Previously, in the history of queen and king relationships, the queen does not get an audience with the king. There does not seem to be much of a relationship between the two. Esther changed that as well. The King eagerly responded to Esther's requests to see him.

Esther is not selfish. She could have kept quiet and looked out only for herself. She risked her crown and throne by taking a stand for an entire culture. Esther could have submitted to doubt and fear. She could have stopped pursuing the right thing because of her personal feelings.

Esther teaches us to keep focused on the bigger goal and to pursue that bigger focus with all that you are.

Never let obstacles stop you from pursuing your goals and dreams. Never let your doubts and fears stop you from standing for someone who cannot take a stand from him or herself. Ask for what you need and let others help you. Pride should never interfere with what you are to achieve and to help others to achieve.

Esther modeled a certain level of excellence which was unanticipated. Esther did not exaggerate her power nor did she overuse it. Esther was the more unlikely candidate to capture the throne, thus reinforcing 'do not judge a person by their looks or socioeconomic status.'

No one voluntarily brings two cultures together. Esther is not different. She did not anticipate the need to create space where two (or more) cultures could come together.

Could you have been Esther? What can you do that resembles Esther's care and concern?

WEEK NINETEEN REFLECTION

1. What is your opinion of Esther? What would you have done if you grew up in her time? Do you realize that she is your age?

____

____

____

____

2. What do you want to do that seems overcome with obstacles? How will you overcome those obstacles? Who will you need to help you to overcome those obstacles?

____

____

____

____

3. What does Esther do that you should emulate? Why?

____

____

____

____

4. What do you admire about Esther? Why?

____

____

____

____

5. How does it feel to be chosen? How does it feel to achieve what you have been chosen to do?

____

____

____

6. Do you know what you dream of? What does it take to achieve those dreams? Who do you know that has done those things? When will you contact them to get their advice about your dream?

____

____

____

____

7. For whom do you take a stand? Why? Who takes a stand for you? Why?

____

____

____

8. What are you concerned about? What is on your mind consistently?

____

____

9. Who does God want you to help? Take a stand for? Why?

10. Could you have been Esther? What can you do that resembles Esther's care and concern? What do you care about? What concerns you? What do you care about? What concerns you? Can you help bring back a culture which has faltered? What are you willing to do? What will you do?

WEEK NINETEEN PROJECT

1. Write an affirmation statement. You use this statement to encourage yourself. You use this statement to relieve yourself of all doubt and fear.

____

____

____

____

____

____

2. Make a list of the hardest things you think you want to achieve. Share this list with your 'Naomi.'

____

____

____

____

____

____

WEEK NINETEEN JOURNAL

WEEK TWENTY

Hannah: A Prayer Warrior

Transparent and Unwavering

1 Samuel 1-2

Hannah is by all definitions a prayer warrior, but we really do not know the power of her prayer or her fervor until Samuel is a grown, rather elder man. Hannah is a woman of integrity who keep promises and prays fervently. So fervently that she is accused of being drunk. Hannah was determined that God would hear her, but with her faith, she believed that God would grant her the prayers she prayed.

Hannah was so focused and diligent that she presented God with a deal: "if You give me a child—a son—then I will give him back to You. He will be raised at the church. He will never cut his hair." Hannah persisted in prayer and in pursuit of God for her desires.

Hannah was bullied, so she prayed.

Hannah was provoked, so she prayed.

Hannah was delayed, so she prayed.

Hannah was accused, so she prayed.

As a teenager, you may be thinking, why should I pray. Is God really listening to me? Why does God care about my concerns? Hannah was not much older than you. In that time frame, women were marrying as early as age 15. While it is in unknown how long she has been married or how old she was is at the time of Samuel's birth, it was clear that she was focused on prayer because of her situation. Prayer does not have a requirement of age. Prayer is the signal of spiritual maturity. Prayer is a conversation. Hannah exhibits that prayer is not perfect. She was accused of being drunk. She kept asking for the same thing—repeatedly.

Hannah answers several popular questions:

1. Is God listening to me?
2. Does God get angry if I ask for the same prayer repeatedly?
3. Does God ever change His mind?
4. Does my prayer have any influence on God's will?
5. What good does my prayer do when God already has a plan for this situation?

God is listening to you. He hears you. He heard Abraham, Hannah, David, Solomon, Samuel, Ruth, Mary, Elizabeth, and Jesus. Most of their prayers were by example. Jesus actually taught us how to pray. In all of those cases, God listened.

Hannah repeated this prayer at least yearly until God answered and granted her prayer. If He was annoyed, He would not have granted her the son. God cannot be annoyed by your prayers.

God has been known to change what we perceive to be His mind. What He really did was modify His will. God intended for Hannah to be Samuel's mother. Hannah was used to demonstrate to us fervent prayer. Hannah demonstrates keeping your word. Hannah shares survival techniques for stormy seasons and mean people.

God can add to and expand His will at any time He desires. Because it is God's will, you do not know until it happens. We tend to question it because God does not do His will on our timing.

God does consider our attitude and our attention in prayer as matters unfold to consider if He will change His will. Who will you be once God grants your prayer and desire? The answer will dictate if you will receive that request or even something that God already planned.

Your prayer means that you are concerned about something and God wants to know what you are concerned about. He considers those things which concern us. So He will listen and this prayer may help you be peaceful while you are waiting on God's perfect will.

Hannah is our prayer warrior. She is transparent and unwavering. She is who we should pattern our prayer life after.

Prayer is powerful. Prayer should be transparent. Prayer should be unwavering.

Pray.

Transparent.

Unwavering.

WEEK TWENTY REFLECTION

1. What is most impressive about Hannah? What will you do in your life based on what Hannah shows you?

____

____

____

____

2. What was powerful about the prayer that Hannah prayed?

____

____

____

____

3. Could you have kept the promise that Hannah made and kept? Why or why not? If not, what will you do so that you can keep your word and fulfill your promises?

____

____

____

____

4. Do you pray? What happens when you pray? Do you have an example of when God has answered your prayer(s)?

____

____

____

____

5. What makes you not pray? What makes you afraid to pray? Who do you know who prays consistently?

____

____

____

____

6. What do you think is worthy of prayer? What is not worthy of prayer?

____

____

____

____

7. How do you make decisions when you don't pray?

____

____

____

____

8. Who will you pray with? When will you pray? What will you pray about?

____

____

____

____

9.   Who will you share your prayer life with?

____

____

____

____

10. Are you able to help others pray?

____

____

____

____

WEEK TWENTY PROJECT

1. Make a prayer list of who and what you need to pray for.

____

____

____

____

____

____

____

____

____

____

____

____

2. Start a separate journal for the promises and the gifts that God gives you, without or with prayer.

WEEK TWENTY JOURNAL

ONE OF MY FAVORITE QUOTES

Some words to live by.

"Our deepest fear is not that we are inadequate. Our deepest fear is that we are powerful beyond measure. It is our light, not our darkness that most frightens us. We ask ourselves, 'Who am I to be brilliant, gorgeous, talented, fabulous?' Actually, who are you not to be? You are a child of God. Your playing small does not serve the world. There is nothing enlightened about shrinking so that other people won't feel insecure around you. We are all meant to shine, as children do. We were born to make manifest the glory of God that is within us. It's not just in some of us; it's in everyone. And as we let our own light shine, we unconsciously give other people permission to do the same. As we are liberated from our own fear, our presence automatically liberates others."

— Marianne Williamson, *A Return to Love: Reflections on the Principles of "A Course in Miracles"*

WEEK TWENTY-ONE

Bathsheba

Situational Sin: When Your Plan to Sin Fails

2 Samuel 11—12

Bathsheba meets David because she was bathing. David was supposed to be at war but he was on the roof. If David had been where he was supposed to be, this sin would have never happened. Bathsheba would have not ever attracted David otherwise. He would not have witnessed her bathing. In the definition of the word, David can see her actual body shape. She was actually bathing. David was attracted to her so he sent someone to find her and discover her identity. For the record, David is handsome and the King of Israel. David can have any woman that he wants. He sends for her and they have sex. That's when the sin occurred. David should not have slept with her; she was another man's wife. For the record, Bathsheba was not able to say no either. It was the King. The sin she committed was situational—she was in a compromising position. There were other consequences to telling the King no. So they had sex—the first sin. Then David tried to cover the sex up—the second sin. Bathsheba is caught up with David, his decisions, and his level of power.

What does that mean for you as a young lady? What are your situational sins—you didn't see the sin coming? You were sitting next to the people who were cheating. They were caught and you were accused.

You were in a relationship with a young man and you had sex because he issued an ultimatum: if you really like me then you will have sex with me. So you did have sex and then you got pregnant. What do you do? You sinned to "save a relationship" but you then had to pay for two sins. You are still responsible for those sins and should repent for those sins, and whose future generations will pay for those sins.

Situational sins occur when we have not considered our company (our friends and family) or the activities which you will engage and participate in as sins and possible sins. If your cousins are gambling at the family reunion, but you did not know that was gambling when you did that same activity at school with your friends, then as a result, your 'situational sin' caused you to be suspended.

There are thousands of people who innocently drove the 'getaway' car from the bank robbery who go to jail or has a criminal history because of the decision of someone else.

Some situational sin is based on our lack of preparation. Ask questions. Say no to people who you do not know. Limit out of the ordinary events or activities which could lead to sin.

Situational sin does not end your life or cause your life to look extremely different but in Bathsheba's life it really changed. Her husband was killed because David wanted to cover up the pregnancy and was unsuccessful in getting the husband to come home and have sex with his wife. After the husband's death, David married Bathsheba. Bathsheba carried that baby to term and birthed it, but God did not allow him to live because of their sin, which was initiated by David. Then once that baby died, Bathsheba and David conceived another son, Solomon.

Was the sin worth it? Was the cover up worth it? Did Bathsheba try to prevent the sin? Did Bathsheba repent? Who did God punish? Who was punished because someone else was punished?

When your plan to sin fails, then you regroup and choose correctly next time. Choose to do the right thing. Avoid sin: situational or otherwise.

Bathsheba was the mother of a great king, so her future was not ruined. Solomon's future was not interrupted.

Sin can be debilitating. Sin can stifle. Sin causes friction. Sin does a lot to each person. Sin can be avoided. Pray. Pray to escape the temptation that so easily entangles us.

Remember that some of the escapes which God provides are narrow, incomprehensible, unrecognizable, and time-sensitive. Take action quickly. Avoiding, ignoring, and overcoming sin is difficult, I agree. You may not get it right every time but try every time and try every day to get it right.

WEEK TWENTY-ONE REFLECTION

1. What are your sins?

____

____

____

____

2. What entices you to sin?

____

____

____

____

3. What events or details stop you from sinning?

____

____

____

____

4. Who gets you in the most trouble? Who do you cause to sin?

____

____

____

5. What will it take for you to stop sinning?

6. Do you ask God for help to stop? Consistently?

7. What was your opinion of Bathsheba because of her sins?

8. What was your opinion of David because of his sins?

9. As Bathsheba, what could she have done differently to avoid the situation?

10. Who was punished because someone else was punished?

WEEK TWENTY-ONE PROJECT

1. Find 5 scriptures which address the escape and the avoidance of sin. (Hint: search for avoiding sin in biblegateway.com)

____

____

____

____

____

____

2. Make a board of the scriptures on index cards so that you can see them daily for recall and remembering.

WEEK TWENTY-ONE JOURNAL

WEEK TWENTY-TWO

Lois and Eunice: A Legacy of Faith

[5] I am reminded of your sincere faith, which first lived in your grandmother Lois and in your mother Eunice and, I am persuaded, now lives in you also.

2 Timothy 1:5

In Hebrews 11, verse one reads that faith is the substance of things hoped for, the evidence of things not seen. Faith is sometimes hard to understand and reconcile. Faith is challenged when what you are believing God for does not happen.

The Bible does not detail how Paul evidence of Lois and Eunice's faith. Paul commends them for being faithful, and more importantly, sharing their faith with Timothy.

So what does faith look like to you? Who has faith that you respect? What does that faith look like? How do they share their faith with you? When was his/her faith made evident to you?

What does faith mean to you? Do others know that you have faith?

What event(s) caused you to question God? Or get close or even doubt or disbelieve God?

One measures faith based on what you see that God delivers. When we get good grades and are blessed with good health then you are a believing and faithful person. When everything is well, your faith is fine.

So the test of your faith shows up when your family is homeless, your parent loses a job, your grades are challenged, your social life is not going well, the death of a loved one, or not being accepted to the college of your choice. While these are just suggestions, they are real issues for someone—someday maybe for you.

What do you do when your faith is tested? Do you seek God or do you run?

Faith is your belief in God and His sovereignty. When you tell God that you want a certain thing but you do not receive that requested in your timing, that does not mean that you will never receive what you requested.

What do you pray for? What are you hoping God will do for you? For your family? For your friends?

Faith is measured how you behave when God does not give your what you want, like you want it, because you want it, when you want it, and what you do as a result of God's delay, changes, or denial.

Death or departure of a loved one is what usually causes the ultimate questions you will pose to God.

Authentic faith requires you to carry on without what you have asked for. Can you live without what God has not given you or the challenges you are presented? Will you continue to love God and serve Him regardless of your circumstances? Can you still believe in God when the 'worst' has seemingly taken place?

Losing a person—when they die—often causes the greatest distance between God and people. God may be questioned most often about why did He take that person. You are usually willing to trade them for someone. But you don't have the big picture, complete picture. God has the big glasses on and He knows why He is taking them from this Earth and you.

Just a note of wisdom: be careful of asking God 'why me?' His answer will change your life and often causes you to come closer to Him at an unexpected time. What He has the opportunity to reveal is heart-warming and ground shaking. One of His responses is: Why not you? Are you ready for that and all that comes with that question? Please also understand that the answer that God provides does not normally solve your personal situation.

Is there any reasonable explanation for 'why did You take my grandmother away from me while all of the adults in my life are being foolish?' Not one which causes you the resolve that you seek. God may intend to grow you up and cause you to expose the reality of your situation but grandmother was shielding you from the reality. She was also very sick and the pain was unbearable, which she also shielded you from. God took care of all of that. But you and the church pray for healing, believing that she would be healed and present for your next birthday. Is it better for her to receive her request or yours?

Trusting in God and having faith means that we accept what He does and carry on.

Faith is a tall order. It requires undiscovered Christian maturity and your faith increases with every opportunity God presents or allows. Faith is only strengthened through trial, just like muscle is strengthened through exercise, which is why you may hear the term: an exercise of your faith.

These increases in faith often come before a new assignment, which requires this increased faith. Lois and Eunice were Timothy's legacy of faith which Timothy needed to carry out his work which Paul was leaving for him to do.

Peter was tested to increase his faith because he was about to walk into unchartered territory. Hebrews 11 lists several examples of the faith of those God has called and how they represented with faith.

It is your job to do the same. Despite all of your situations and seemingly misfortunes, seek faith. Seek faith in God because He provides those situations so that we can grow and have a testimony to share and to help someone else grow!

Faith stimulates growth and growth affirms trust. Trust means God is giving us what He wants and maybe what we want.

Faith: essential, difficult, complex, complicated, profound, prolific, outrageous, and outlandish.

WEEK TWENTY-TWO

1. How do you define faith?

____

____

____

____

2. Who has faith that you respect? What does that faith look like?

____

____

____

____

3. How do others share their faith with you?

____

____

____

____

4. When was his/her faith made evident to you?

____

____

____

5. What does faith mean to you?

6. Do others know that you have faith? How do they know?

7. Are there events which caused you to question God? Explain. Or get close to questioning God? Doubt God? Disbelieve in God? Explain.

8. What do you want God to give you that He has not yet given you? Can you live without that?

9. Will you continue to love God and serve God regardless of your circumstances?

10. Can you still believe in God and believe God when seemingly the worst has happened?

11. Have you ever asked God 'why is this happening to me?' What did God say? How did that make you feel? What are you going to do if God says 'why not you?'

12. What will it take for you to have great faith?

13. How would you grade your faith on a scale of 1-10, 10 being the best? What can you do to improve that number?

WEEK TWENTY-TWO PROJECT

1. Review Hebrews 11 below. Highlight the story/person you most admire. Write a goal that you have/will ask God to make a reality. Put the date on the goal of the day you prayer about it.

Hebrews 11 New International Version (NIV)

Faith in Action

11 Now faith is confidence in what we hope for and assurance about what we do not see. [2] This is what the ancients were commended for.

[3] By faith we understand that the universe was formed at God's command, so that what is seen was not made out of what was visible.

[4] By faith Abel brought God a better offering than Cain did. By faith he was commended as righteous, when God spoke well of his offerings. And by faith Abel still speaks, even though he is dead.

[5] By faith Enoch was taken from this life, so that he did not experience death: "He could not be found, because God had taken him away." For before he was taken, he was commended as one who pleased God. [6] And without faith it is impossible to please God, because anyone who comes to him must believe that he exists and that he rewards those who earnestly seek him.

[7] By faith Noah, when warned about things not yet seen, in holy fear built an ark to save his family. By his faith he condemned the world and became heir of the righteousness that is in keeping with faith.

[8] By faith Abraham, when called to go to a place he would later receive as his inheritance, obeyed and went, even though he did not know where he was going. [9] By faith he made his home in the promised land like a stranger in a foreign country; he lived in tents, as did Isaac and Jacob, who were heirs with him of the same promise. [10] For he was looking forward to the city with foundations, whose architect and builder is God. [11] And by faith even Sarah, who was past childbearing age, was enabled to bear children because she considered him faithful who had made the

promise. [12] And so from this one man, and he as good as dead, came descendants as numerous as the stars in the sky and as countless as the sand on the seashore.

[13] All these people were still living by faith when they died. They did not receive the things promised; they only saw them and welcomed them from a distance, admitting that they were foreigners and strangers on earth. [14] People who say such things show that they are looking for a country of their own. [15] If they had been thinking of the country they had left, they would have had opportunity to return. [16] Instead, they were longing for a better country—a heavenly one. Therefore God is not ashamed to be called their God, for he has prepared a city for them.

[17] By faith Abraham, when God tested him, offered Isaac as a sacrifice. He who had embraced the promises was about to sacrifice his one and only son, [18] even though God had said to him, "It is through Isaac that your offspring will be reckoned." [19] Abraham reasoned that God could even raise the dead, and so in a manner of speaking he did receive Isaac back from death.

[20] By faith Isaac blessed Jacob and Esau in regard to their future.

[21] By faith Jacob, when he was dying, blessed each of Joseph's sons, and worshiped as he leaned on the top of his staff.

[22] By faith Joseph, when his end was near, spoke about the exodus of the Israelites from Egypt and gave instructions concerning the burial of his bones.

[23] By faith Moses' parents hid him for three months after he was born, because they saw he was no ordinary child, and they were not afraid of the king's edict.

[24] By faith Moses, when he had grown up, refused to be known as the son of Pharaoh's daughter. [25] He chose to be mistreated along with the people of God rather than to enjoy the fleeting pleasures of sin. [26] He regarded disgrace for the sake of Christ as of greater value than the treasures of Egypt, because he was looking ahead to his reward. [27] By faith he left Egypt, not fearing the king's anger; he persevered because he saw him who is invisible. [28] By faith he

kept the Passover and the application of blood, so that the destroyer of the firstborn would not touch the firstborn of Israel.

[29] By faith the people passed through the Red Sea as on dry land; but when the Egyptians tried to do so, they were drowned.

[30] By faith the walls of Jericho fell, after the army had marched around them for seven days.

[31] By faith the prostitute Rahab, because she welcomed the spies, was not killed with those who were disobedient.

[32] And what more shall I say? I do not have time to tell about Gideon, Barak, Samson and Jephthah, about David and Samuel and the prophets, [33] who through faith conquered kingdoms, administered justice, and gained what was promised; who shut the mouths of lions,[34] quenched the fury of the flames, and escaped the edge of the sword; whose weakness was turned to strength; and who became powerful in battle and routed foreign armies. [35] Women received back their dead, raised to life again. There were others who were tortured, refusing to be released so that they might gain an even better resurrection. [36] Some faced jeers and flogging, and even chains and imprisonment. [37] They were put to death by stoning; they were sawed in two; they were killed by the sword. They went about in sheepskins and goatskins, destitute, persecuted and mistreated— [38] the world was not worthy of them. They wandered in deserts and mountains, living in caves and in holes in the ground.

[39] These were all commended for their faith, yet none of them received what had been promised, [40] since God had planned something better for us so that only together with us would they be made perfect.

____

____

____

____

____

____

2. Read one of these Biblical accounts. Summarize the faith which was embodied. How would you have responded or behaved.

1 Samuel 1-2

Luke 1:26-56

Luke 1:57-80

WEEK TWENTY-TWO JOURNAL

WEEK TWENTY THREE

Lydia: Being First Has Its Benefits

Sharing Jesus With Others

Lydia's Conversion in Philippi

[11] From Troas we put out to sea and sailed straight for Samothrace, and the next day we went on to Neapolis. [12] From there we traveled to Philippi, a Roman colony and the leading city of that district of Macedonia. And we stayed there several days.
[13] On the Sabbath we went outside the city gate to the river, where we expected to find a place of prayer. We sat down and began to speak to the women who had gathered there. [14] One of those listening was a woman from the city of Thyatira named Lydia, a dealer in purple cloth. She was a worshiper of God. The Lord opened her heart to respond to Paul's message. [15] When she and the members of her household were baptized, she invited us to her home. "If you consider me a believer in the Lord," she said, "come and stay at my house." And she persuaded us.

Acts 16:11-15

Lydia was the first amongst in Philippi to accept Christ. She also shared Jesus with her family. She and her family were also baptized. She invited Paul and Silas to her home. They visited them to encourage them. Lydia is credited for being the first Christian in her area, which led to Christianity to America. While that may be slightly looser and less detailed than the actual account, realize that she shared Jesus and was receptive when Jesus was shared with her and her family.

Who is responsible for you knowing Christ and God? When did you first hear about God? How would you know about God if you were never invited to Church or someone never shared God with you? There are times when you should and will reflect on who first introduced you to Christ. That moment should cause you great joy. You should realize that all the events leading up to that point will now make so much more sense. Was your family a part of your conversion? Did you ever thank that person for being obedient and brave enough for introducing you to God and Jesus Christ and the Holy Spirit? What did you do next after the conversion? Did you share your conversion with your family? Did you share your conversion with your friends? Are you obedient and brave enough to share Jesus with others? What will it take to share Jesus with others?

Lydia took the risk that God provided for her to follow Him and be converted. Her story is special because she violated some customs regarding inviting men to her home. Remember also that she was a woman—the prohibition on women speaking and having influence and exercising that influence is prohibited. She was not supposed to do that, so her voice was not supposed to be heard. Lydia may have given others the courage to do the same: boldly accept and share God and Jesus Christ with others.

What does Lydia do that inspires you to share Jesus?

Sharing Jesus is scary? Yes, it is. If you introduce Jesus to someone, they may judge you or get uncomfortable with you. You may lose a friend. That person may avoid you in the future. So when you share Jesus, please pray. Don't quit. Don't pre-judge. Most importantly, realize that the biggest risk taker is God. God provides the platform for sharing, the person and the location. God risked your obedience and not yielding to fear of rejection. God takes the actual risk, not you. If the person says no, then the person actually rejected God and Jesus—not you. So be careful when you deciding not to share Jesus because the person may not reject you. You cannot make that decision for God. God has to change the messenger when don't do your job. If you don't share Jesus when you are designed to, then when will Jesus get someone else to do your assignment?

Part of this assignment for you is to build confidence in you to share the gospel. Can you tell someone else that you are a member of a church and that you believe in Jesus? Then you progress form that sharing of how you come to know Christ personally, inclusive of how you have grown since you accepted His protection, love and salvation.

After that, then you are presented with the opportunity to share Jesus and lead them to Christ. You do not need to be perfect at sharing. Just start with 'do you know Jesus?' Then just go to inviting them to church or give them an online church service or a church DVD so that they can hear the message.

Remember sharing Jesus is just a conversation. You are not asking any questions. You are sharing what you know. Once they actually accept Christ and join church, they will be given more detailed information. Sharing Jesus also means trusting God to carry out His complete plan and to use you to do it. It is awesome to share and they come back with the story of acceptance.

Someone shared with you. Who will you share with? What will happen when presented with the opportunity to share?

WEEK TWENTY-THREE REFLECTION

1. Who is responsible for you knowing Christ and God?

____

____

____

2. When did you first hear about God?

____

____

____

3. How would you know about God if you were never invited to church or someone never shared God with you?

____

____

____

4. Was your family involved in your conversion? Explain. Are they converted as well?

____

____

____

____

5. What did you do next after the conversion? Did you share your conversion with your family?

____

____

____

6. Did you share your conversion with your friends? How? What was their reaction?

____

____

____

7. Are you obedient and brave enough to share Jesus with others? What will it take to share Jesus with others?

____

____

____

8. What does Lydia do that inspires you to share Jesus?

____

____

9. What is the scariest part of sharing? What are you afraid of?

10. If you don't share when you are designed to share then how will they learn of Jesus? Who will God assign in your spot?

11. How do you think you will know you need to share?

WEEK TWENTY-THREE PROJECT

1. Make a list of friends and family that you know for sure that do not know Jesus or you are uncertain about their relationship with God and Jesus Christ.

2. Make a plan to share. Include what you would say, scriptures you will share, and a prayer that you can pray.

____

____

____

____

____

____

____

____

____

____

____

____

____

____

____

WEEK TWENTY-THREE JOURNAL

WEEK TWENTY-FOUR

Mary: A Life Worthy of Being Called

Luke 1:26-56, 2

[29] Mary was greatly troubled at his words and wondered what kind of greeting this might be. [30] But the angel said to her, "Do not be afraid, Mary; you have found favor with God. [31] You will conceive and give birth to a son, and you are to call him Jesus. [32] He will be great and will be called the Son of the Most High. The Lord God will give him the throne of his father David, [33] and he will reign over Jacob's descendants forever; his kingdom will never end."

Luke 1:29-33

Mary.

A Virgin.

Promised to be married.

Teenager.

Probably good grades if there was school.

Honorable mention.

Chosen.

Biggest assignment next to one Jesus had Himself.

To be the mother of Jesus.

Everybody has a mom. Everyone needs a mom. Famous people have moms—some of which are not famous but because of who she parents, she is now famous. Imagine one day that your mother's life changes because you dunk a basketball, the songs you sing play on the radio all day, you are elected to public office, or you win the Pulitzer prize or the Super Bowl. Your mother's life will change as well.

But none of that has anything to do with how Mary was chosen. She is your typical teenager with a promise to marry a man who is older yet is visited by an angel who told him that she will be giving birth to a Son who will be named Immanuel. Several questions are reasonable and imminent: 1) Why me? 2) How is this possible? 3) Why me? 4) What do I do next? 5) Why me? 6) How do I tell my parents? 7) Why me? 8) Why me? 9) Why me? 10) Why me?

Teenage pregnancy is embarrassing now but back then you could be stoned to death. It was a family embarrassment and your family would be outcast. If your family had a business, it may be forced to close due to lack of business. Your parent may be fired from his job because of your behavior. In addition, you are engaged to be married so now his family is embarrassed as well.

But God chose Mary! So those details have been handled. Crisis averted. It was not easy but God handled it all because it was God's divine will.

Mary could handle the assignment. God chose her and created her for that very assignment. She was faithful and obedient, receptive, sensitive and a servant of God.

She probably did not ask 'why me' as many times as written here, as you would have, but she carefully suggests that she will need an explanation of the situation. So Mary is chosen. What do you want to be chosen for? What do you want to be worthy of being chosen for? What will your choices prevent or decide that you will do? Do you realize that today's choices determine what your future will afford you? Mary had apparently done pretty well with behavior and attitude and whatever the criteria God used to select Mary.

College admissions is a topic which is relevant to this discussion. You have dreamed of attending a particular college. This dream included a scholarship. When you applied to school, you were waitlisted. Upon further investigation into why you were waitlisted, then you realized that you did not take a high enough level math class. Rather than taking Pre-Calculus, you took Math Models. At the time you decided to take Math Models, you were not knowledgeable about the college entrance requirements. Now you do not have the four math credits which are required to enter college because you took the less challenging path. To rectify that error in judgement and the relaxed work ethic, you have to attend summer school to take the same class you had planned to avoid. In addition to all of that, you missed out on the scholarships as well. All because of one wrong move, which did not look or feel all that wrong at the time. Further, no one advised against it, except for that one teacher, but you just thought that she was being difficult; no one loves math like she does.

Are you worthy to be chosen? What does God want you to do? What has He chosen you to do? What do you want God to choose you for?

Mary did not try to hide her situation nor did she deny God. She lived through the entire situation. She grew closer to God in this situation. Mary sought wisdom by visiting Elizabeth. She did not complain. She did not try to run from God's assignment. If she ever said that she totally belonged to God and that she surrendered all, then she meant it. God believed her.

Can you say anything like that? Can you do that? Can God trust you to do what He has chosen you to do?

Mary is your example of how to carry out God's plan with all the distractions and disruptions around you. You will need this example and support. It is a noisy world out there. Sometimes it is hard to see God in your situation because there are so many distractions. Sometimes it is hard to hear God in your life because your music is so loud.

Adjust your life to be worthy of being chosen.

WEEK TWENTY-FOUR REFLECTION

1. What would have been your reaction if you had been Mary? What is our opinion of Mary?

____

____

____

____

2. What do you want God to choose you for?

____

____

____

3. What do you think God has chosen you for?

____

____

____

4. What are you doing that you never imagined you would?

____

____

____

5. What do you need to do to correct aspects of your life which challenges your ability to be chosen?

____

____

____

____

6. What has He chosen you for which you are trying to avoid?

____

____

____

____

7. What do you need to modify so that you can hear from God?

____

____

____

____

8. What do you need to alter so that you can see the hand of God?

____

____

____

9. Can God trust you to do His work according to His will? What will it take for you to arrive there?

10. What has God already done in your life which makes you resemble and/or feel like Mary?

WEEK TWENTY-FOUR PROJECT

1. Take a spiritual gift inventory. https://spiritualgiftstest.com/spiritual-gifts-test-youth-version/ if you did not do it in Week Seven. What are your gifts? What should you do with those gifts?

____

____

____

____

____

2. Make a poster displaying those gifts and where you could use the gifts.

3. Add your dreams to your vision board.

WEEK TWENTY-FOUR JOURNAL

WEEK TWENTY-FIVE

The Issue of Blood:

A Dogmatic Perseverance and Without the Issue of Image

[42] As Jesus was on his way, the crowds almost crushed him. [43] And a woman was there who had been subject to bleeding for twelve years, but no one could heal her. [44] She came up behind him and touched the edge of his cloak, and immediately her bleeding stopped.
[45] "Who touched me?" Jesus asked.
When they all denied it, Peter said, "Master, the people are crowding and pressing against you."
[46] But Jesus said, "Someone touched me; I know that power has gone out from me."
[47] Then the woman, seeing that she could not go unnoticed, came trembling and fell at his feet. In the presence of all the people, she told why she had touched him and how she had been instantly healed. [48] Then he said to her, "Daughter, your faith has healed you. Go in peace."

Luke 8:42b-48

This woman had an affliction which caused her to bleed for over 12 years! Consistently. Constantly. Without end. With no cure. Without a break. This is not the same as your monthly cycle. This is an ongoing flow which is annoying and possibly painful, inconvenient and brings judgment, and just down right embarrassing.

What is your issue of blood? What do you have going on in your life that embarrasses you or that causes you angst? What do you wish you did not have to endure?

The woman serves as an example for us. Let's examine her situation. She was sick—ill. Because of her illness, she was considered unclean. Have you ever sat next to someone that you hope does not accidentally even brush up against you even if ever so slightly? Maybe they smell or their clothes are dirty or tattered. Whatever it is that is visible to you is not pleasing to you. Understand that is this time period, she is not only unclean, she is completely unwelcomed. She is not supposed to be around people so the first thing is that she broke a rule. Now she broke a rule in order to reach Jesus. Was it worth the risk? Is it worth the risk required to seek God?

The woman heard about Jesus. She had spent ALL of her money on available earthly treatments—all of which had failed. Now, she seeks the Healer because she heard what He had done. She made a decision to trust God.

So she decided to seek Jesus. She decided to break the law. She decided that if only she could touch Jesus' garment that she would be healed.

She was ill; in pain but she still walked all the way to Jesus. She did not stop or get lost. She walked—she did not catch an Uber or cab. She walked to Jesus, fought through a crowd, to touch His hem of His cloak.

How did she know that His power existed in His clothing? How did she know that His power would transfer to her?

She didn't actually know but she BELIEVED that it would. She was willing to trust Him. She had exhausted all other options. All that was left was this new option: Jesus. This revelation required faith again.

So what do you to defy societal measures and standards in order to achieve some faith based results? What is your faith requiring you to do? What are your circumstances requiring you to do?

So the woman pressed through the crowd, unclean, made her way to Jesus because she desired heading and was determined to be healed, and touched the hem of His garment.

Jesus felt the power leave His body. Wow! The power that left His body He could feel it?! That is amazing! With so much power, how could that seemingly small percentage leave and be noticed? Well, the power she 'stole' healed her immediately! She was healed upon the transfer of the noticed power.

She was healed! All of her efforts paid off. The crowd was gigantic and they were aggressive. They were there for the same reason that she was: Jesus. But none had her perseverance or tenacity. She actually intentionally touched Him, with a purpose, for a reason, with a faith that required perseverance. What would you do next? Now?

Well then the disciples were confused. Jesus asked them who touched Him. They are not good crowd control people. They are supposed to know who has been close to Jesus but they have failed. Jesus persisted and explained. This time she came forward. She confessed. Then she said it, "It was me." Jesus looked upon her with compassion and declared that her faith had healed her. He then commended her to go in peace. What do you when Jesus speaks to you?

She was trying to go away unnoticed but she was still close enough to hear Him ask who touched me. Why? Why hadn't she been running through the crowd celebrating and testifying? Or at least out of hearing range?

Why would God save and heal you for you to go unnoticed?

Now that Jesus knows who was healed, now what does that mean?

Jesus healed us for a few reasons: because it is God's will, He needs your testimony, and He will get the glory. When all of this is done, Jesus has accomplished what He was called us to do: Draw all men and women to Himself.

She did not quit.

She broke the law.

She violated the cultural and societal norms.

She acknowledged His power. She was willing to submit to His will. She surrendered totally to Jesus. She did all of through actions. She did not talk about it. She did it. She made up her mind. She got dressed. She left home. She worked through the crowd. She made it to Jesus. She touched His clothes. She was healed. He declared that her faith had healed her. She celebrated inside. All of this happened in public, with an audience. She could have quit at each step. We might have quit. But she did not. She was healed because she persecuted and did not quit. She did not stop.

Jesus affirmed her. Jesus excused and celebrated her 'stolen' power. She did not leave guilty of what she had done. Jesus loved her and lifted her head.

She stopped being concerned about the image and the societal and cultural norms and standards. She started living when she started seeking Jesus—with a dogmatic perseverance.

Now that she is healed she is probably popular, but that no longer matters. She is living for what matters to God now. Jesus changed her life, her situations, and her circumstances. He really changed her perspective.

WEEK TWENTY-FIVE REFLECTION

1. What is your opinion of this woman? How would you handle her situation if it were yours?

____

____

____

2. How would you feel? Scared? Overwhelmed? Distraught? Peaceful? Calm? Courageous?

____

____

____

3. What numerical value would you assign to her faith? How does it compare to yours?

____

____

____

4. What can you do that is outrageous and outlandish which demonstrates your faith in God, Jesus and the Holy Spirit?

____

____

5. What is your 'issue of blood'? Family? Health? Grades? Social? Future? Relationships?

6. What does Jesus want/expect for you to do about your 'issue'? What are going to do?

7. Who are you going to ask to pray with you? Who are you going to tell when your 'issue' is solved?

8. What did she inspire you to do/achieve/attempt?

9. How did your connection to Jesus increase once reading what He did?

10. What will He do for you based on what He did for her?

11. What would you have done after the healing?

WEEK TWENTY-FIVE PROJECT

Make a list of your prayer requests. Attach a scripture to each of your requests.

WEEK TWENTY-FIVE JOURNAL

WEEK TWENTY-SIX

Work Ethic

[23] Whatever you do, work at it with all your heart, as working for the Lord, not for human masters,

Colossians 3:23

Work ethic is defined as your ability to do something such as work, clean your room, study, get good grades, etc., with the maximum amount of effort, which should also yield the best possible results.

As a teenager, developing a great work ethic will yield life-long results. Keep in mind that your parents have a responsibility to teach you healthy work ethic but you also have to learn that work ethic and use that work ethic. Daily. For the rest of your life.

The hardest word to recover from is the label of lazy. Never earn that label! No matter what you do! Work ethic is important because you need to be able to finish something, hopefully everything you start.

Work ethic helps you to achieve your goals. It is what distinguishes you from others who want what you want but are not willing to work to go get it.

Consider the list of goals you have for yourself. A popular goal is to be a lawyer/attorney. In order to be an attorney, you need a bachelor's degree, so that's four years of college. You need an LSAT of 165. You need to be admitted into law school. Attend for three years. During law school, you will read tens of thousands of pages. That seven years requires work ethic. You cannot quit or stall or delay.

When you graduate at 25 years old, you them know what is required to understand how to manage life and all of its details.

Work ethic sharpens your integrity. You develop character through working. Work ethic also keeps you focused on the task at hand.

In high school, you have homework. That homework is training for college. If you never had homework in high school, the college workload would be massive. You may feel that you could not make it. Matriculating through college requires work ethic and hopefully it does not have to be developed at the risk of some grades.

Work ethic is a reputation. You want to be known for completing your work and giving it the best that you are. Neat. Organized. On-time. Effort.

Are you a good student? Why or why not? What do your teachers think of you? Do you know that they judge who you are based on what you produce in their classroom? Do you know that they judge who you are going to be based on the work that you produce in their classroom? Is that fair? Yes and no. You are judged by the work that you produce. Is it fair? Yes and no. Based on what you do will determine what decision makers will allow you to do next.

Suppose your 9th grade year was terrible so your grades suffered, those grades cause you to miss qualifications for the National Honor Society in your 11th grade year. That is the judgment which exists, even though you have made great progress since then. Is that fair? No. You may not been in control of those issues which caused your grades to suffer.

One might argue that nothing should interfere with your performance, that you should be able to still do your work regardless of your circumstances. That is easier said than done. Those circumstances are personal to you. Coping with those circumstances are also personal to you. So you need to consider the future, residual consequences for those situations.

The good news is that a college personal statement will allow you to share the details of your situation and the outcomes which resulted.

On the other side of this is the story of the student who made excellent grades with your same circumstances. Always consider that. Learn to ask for help. At any time.

Consider the label of hard worker. Determine what is required to earn that label. Do what is required until you earn that label then continue. Daily.

Work ethic is a matter of trust. Can you be trusted to complete the assigned task? Will you do it with only the resources provided? Not spend more than is allocated? Not cheating?

Consider work ethic reputation as it relates to college admittance and scholarships. Suppose you are admitted and given a full scholarship, your entire education, room fees and food, all paid for. This college is one of the top universities—amongst the best in the nation. You go to school but you do not do you work or pass your exams. Your grades cause you to be on academic probation. Consider that you were trusted to do well at school because of your previous grades. Now you have actually wasted money that could have been used for someone else to attend the school or for something else that your guardian needed.

That university made an investment in you because of your demonstrated work ethic.

People will judge you based on what you do now for your potential later.

There have been 45 presidents elected that position since the inception of this counting. They have various backgrounds, social statuses and reputations. Based on their actions while in office, determines if they are reelected. There was one president who was so well liked and so good at the job that he was reelected three times, serving a total of 4 terms, 16 years. It is because of Theodore "Teddy" Roosevelt that the Congress voted in the 22nd Amendment which limits presidential terms to 2 terms, 8 years. This does not include any years which you inherited the office due to the sitting president vacating the office.

All of these presidents had teachers, college professors, and advisors who knew their work ethic. When the 44th President took office someone counted the minimum number of teachers that he could have had. The number was about 100. That should be 100 automatic votes for the office election. Your teachers should be your advocate. They invested in you. They saw potential that you were not aware of. They are not surprised when you achieve big things.

Do your teachers feel that way about you? Does your family feel that way about you? Do you feel that way about yourself?

How would grade your work ethic? Do you feel prepared to be successful in the world? What does it take to reach that in your life? How do you define work ethic? Who has the best work ethic that you know? What did they do to make you pay attention to their work ethic? What are you going to do to impress them with yours?

Why is work ethic important? What does it mean to you? How will you improve your attitude?

WEEK TWENTY-SIX REFLECTION

1. What have you done today to invest in your future? If nothing, why not?

____

____

____

____

2. Define work ethic. Who taught you the work ethic that you have?

____

____

____

____

3. Are you a good student? Why or why not?

____

____

____

____

4. What do your teachers think of you? How do you know? Is that real or perceived? Based on what specific situations?

____

____

____

____

5. Do you know that they judge who you are based on what you produce in their classroom? Do you know that they judge who you are going to be based on the work that you produce in their classroom? Is it fair that you are judged by the work that you produce? What should you be judged on?

____

____

____

6. How do you define work ethic? What does it mean to you? How would grade your work ethic?

____

____

____

7. Who has the best work ethic that you know? What did they do to make you pay attention to their work ethic? What are you going to do to impress them with yours?

____

____

____

8. Do you feel prepared to be successful in the world? What does it take to reach that in your life?

____

____

____

____

9. Why is work ethic important? What does it mean to you? How will you improve your attitude?

____

____

____

10. Do your teachers feel that you have work ethic which they could support publicly? Does your family feel that way about you? Do you feel that way about yourself?

____

____

____

WEEK TWENTY-SIX PROJECT

1. Vision Board Addition

Goals with Dates: What does it take today to achieve those goals?

College

Career

More Education

Extravagant Goal

2. Who will you share your vision board with?

____

____

____

____

WEEK TWENTY-SIX JOURNAL

WEEK TWENTY-SEVEN

With Zeal, Pursue and Proceed

[16] So, because you are lukewarm—neither hot nor cold—I am about to spit you out of my mouth.

Revelation 3:16

[13] I can do all this through him who gives me strength.

Philippians 4:13

[2] Consider it pure joy, my brothers and sisters, whenever you face trials of many kinds, [3] because you know that the testing of your faith produces perseverance. [4] Let perseverance finish its work so that you may be mature and complete, not lacking anything.

James 1:2-4

With zeal. Zest. Enthusiasm. Passion. Excitement. Joy. Drive. Determination. Exhilaration. Eagerness. Earnestness. Emotion. Energy. Fierceness. Frenzy. Intensity. Intentionally.

Pursue the ideas and the required activities with passion. One of the long standing complaints about teenagers is that you all are lazy. Lazy includes the phrase 'I'm not doing that.' What <u>will</u> you do? Lazy starts with a mentality—one where you decide to do something which adds to or changes the course of your life. What do we want you to do? Pursue a life of excellence! Excellence means the best attitude, with the best work ethic.

School is attached to your future. What do you want it to resemble? Based on that future dream destination, determines what you need to strive for. Entrance into Stanford, LSU, Notre Dame, Rice, and Howard requires high grades, high SAT scores, and great letters of recommendations. That is a daily task. However, when you are the doctor, lawyer, teacher, athlete, all of that 'sacrifice' will have been worth it. Every day. Excellence. Is. Required.

School is not hard. Tedious, maybe. But necessary. Decide to work hard! Take a short break. Absolutely, but never quit! There is an adage (a wise saying) which says that 'I would rather you have it and not need it, than to need it and not have it.' That means that it is better to have the highest possible grade point average (gpa) so that you can capitalize on all that the high gpa affords you, rather than someone tell you that you would have qualified for a $40,000 scholarship if your gpa was a tenth of a point (0.1) higher. That 0.1 represents one higher grade in one class. So one homework assignment, a better test grade, the retest for a low test grade, or the extra credit that you failed to complete because you did not feel like it. Success starts with effort; you have to make some.

Pursue your education with zeal and zest—give it more than all that you have!

Your behavior—teenage behavior. Difficult. Complicated. Emotional. Temperamental. Fickle. Erratic. Inconsistent.

You respond in some of the most irrational ways which others don't understand and you can't even explain. It is unnerving. Adults are barely able to survive you and your presence and your moods. Your behavior should not offend others. Your behavior should not disrupt the lives of others. Your behavior does not need to cause your parents and guardians to come up with creative punishments when you do the wrong thing. Making poor choices requires the response of others, starting with your parents.

Your behavior is about character. Who are you when no one is watching and what will you do when those who you are accountable for are not present or seemingly not watching? Who are you when you are out front or on stage or being watched? Your character determines your behavior. Character develops over time. Character is groomed over time. Character is measured by your behavior and your attitude and your presentation.

Character means not lying, not stealing, no sex, no drugs, no alcohol, no cheating, no skipping class, not talking back, no disobedience. Character compels you to clean your room, wash your clothes, wash the dishes, do your homework, fold and hang your clothes, wipe the table, sweep the floor, organize the material items which belong to you, and whatever else is necessary at your house—all without being begged or told to do. What do you avoid, but should do? Why do you have an attitude—you reject the request in your heart—when your parents asks you to do anything? Why aren't you willing to participate in your life?

Your best behavior includes not embarrassing your parents and family with your actions. You don't want to be embarrassed, so don't embarrass the family, friends, and community, which works so hard to serve you.

Your best future: what do you dream of? What career have you always talked about? What do you want to do to help others? What is your dream life? What does it take to achieve that? Why do you want it? What are you willing to do to get it?

In Revelation 3:16, God wants a decisive you—not a wishy-washy, change your mind hourly, or indecisive you. Lukewarm means that you are neither hot nor cold. Lukewarm could mean stale. Lukewarm means that you don't have a stance on either side. Lukewarm means your position has not been make plain. It also means that once you do decide, your decision can be changed easily.

If you are not hot, passionate, zealous, excited, determined, enthusiastic, or driven for yourself then nobody will believe that you will invest in anything else at a higher level. Do you think so? Do you agree? So if you don't feel that you should be zealous, determined, driven about your life? Why not?

Don't be lukewarm about your life. Please understand that you cannot expect others to be excited about your life if you are not. Keep that in mind at all times that people will help you at your pace. Get excited about your life! Stop being lukewarm. Your future depends on your zest, excitement, zeal and your drive.

Philippians 4:13 says that 'I can do all things through Him who gives me strength.' You can do it if you let God do it. You cannot achieve anything it you don't start. You cannot have an awesome life if you do not do something toward it daily.

God strengthens your effort, not your laziness or lukewarm disposition. Your future starts with what you do today. So what have you done today to invest in your future?

Lastly, James 1:2-12 summed up as you should have a great attitude and disposition as you go through life. Let's look at the text. Consider it joy when you have trials. You are not the first person who said what and how when they read this. This means to take your trials seriously but with joy to the end of the trial because of the outcome. Receive the trial with excitement; with an attitude of joy; anticipating what God will do with what you have learned from this trial.

Trials are training for perseverance. Perseverance is defined as a steady persistence in a course of action, a purpose, a state, etc., especially in spite of difficulties, obstacles, or discouragement. Perseverance is synonymous to tenacity, persistence, and endurance. It means that you won't give up or quit.

Gold goes through fire to become gold. You have to go through something to become stronger. Trials teach you how to work through problems, how to negotiate, how to not quit, and how to overcome your trials. You learn and mature through trials.

Verse 12 read, "Blessed is the one who perseveres under trial because, having stood the test, that person will receive the crown of life that the Lord has promised to those who love Him." God cannot reward quitters. You cannot quit and get the same reward or praise as if you had finished the race.

There is only rewards for finishing.

Best attitude means that you are still pleasant no matter what the situation.

As a teenager, you may have a bad attitude, or at least that is what every other adult says about you, but you do not know what that means.

Attitude is defined as manner, disposition (neutral, mental, and emotional outlook or mood), feeling, position, etc., with regard to a person or thing. Attitude is what you think or feel about a person, place or thing. So attitude can be positive and negative. Your negative attitude will always be the highlight though. The adults will focus on that. Fair or not does not matter. Why does that matter? Your attitude is what drives you. Your attitude is what causes people to be drawn to you or be repelled from you. While this common knowledge, it is not common practice.

People treat you according to your attitude and what they can expect from you when you speak and respond to what is and done to you. While this could be unfortunate, it is true and real.

How do you 'fix' your attitude? It is not simple, but it is possible. First, control your thoughts. Don't let anyone else control your thoughts or dictate how those thoughts develop. This is difficult because your thoughts are infiltrated 24/7 by social media, and all of the communication apps on your phone. Have you ever considered how hard it is on your immediate family for you to go upstairs happy, only to come back downstairs distraught? It is hard—HARD! Nobody is ever ready for the storm you come out of your room with.

Your family loves you and fights daily to protect you from the ills and evils of this world, sometimes that means protection from yourself.

Your attitude is not going to be perfect or always positive but you should seek it to be positive 90% of the time. Let's discuss that 10%.

There are 'attitude' rules that you should consider.

Nothing foolish. Don't let your attitude cost you anything or anyone.

Nothing permanent. Don't let your attitude make permanent decisions for you.

Nothing deadly. Don't let your attitude cause you to find yourself in a life or death situation.

Nothing embarrassing. Don't let your attitude cause your children to be ashamed of you.

A bad attitude causes others to consider that you are at high risk for being unsuccessful or will ruin the success that you achieve.

So it looks like sucking your teeth, rolling your eyes, disrespectful sighs, slamming doors, talking back and stomping around is unacceptable. This is a short list. However, a bad attitude includes closed body language: folded arms, bowed head, crossed legs, and unpleasant facial expressions.

Attitude is determined by your circumstances but you control that response. Learn to and decide to control your attitude to your benefit.

Is God pleased with the attitude of someone He created in His image? Is He pleased with your attitude? Final note: your parent had a bad day too but manages to ask you about yours in a caring and pleasant manner. Could you respond in a warm, caring and pleasant manner? When you are having the worst day, can you say 'can I have a few minutes/hours/days to respond to that?' rather than have a horrible reaction?

It works. Try it. If it does not work, then email onediagage@onediagage.com to share. We will help you navigate the matter.

Pursue life with zeal, zest, enthusiasm, passion, excitement, joy, drive, determination, exhilaration, eagerness, earnestness, emotion, energy, fierceness, frenzy, intensity, and intentionally.

WEEK TWENTY-SEVEN REFLECTION

1. How would you grade your current effort in your life? Scale 1 to 10; 10 being the best.

2. Are you satisfied with that level? If not, what needs to happen so that you can be satisfied?

3. What will you do?

4. What does it mean to you to pursue a life of excellence?

____

____

5. Where do you want your life to go? Goals: name them.

____

____

____

____

6. What college/university would you like to attend? What are the admission requirements? (Hint: go to the school's website, the admissions tab)

____

____

____

____

7. What are you afraid of? Can that stop you from pursuing a life of excellence? What can we do to prevent that?

____

____

____

____

8. Who are you when no one is watching and what will you do when those who you are accountable for you are not present or seemingly not watching? Who are you when you are out front or on stage or being watched?

____

____

____

____

9. What do you avoid but should do? Why do you have an attitude—you reject the request in your heart—when your parents ask you to do anything? Why aren't you willing to participate in our life?

____

____

____

10. Your best future: what do you dream of? What career have you always talked about? What do you want to do to help others? What is your dream life? What does it take to achieve that? Why do you want it? What are you willing to do to get it?

____

____

____

11. If you are not hot, passionate, zealous, excited, determined, enthusiastic, or driven for yourself then nobody will believe that you will invest in anything else at a higher level. Do you think so? Do you agree? So if you don't feel that you should be zealous, determined, driven about your life, then why not?

____

____

____

____

12. What have you done today to invest in your future?

____

____

____

____

13. Is God pleased with the attitude of someone He created in His image? Is He pleased with your attitude? Final note: your parent had a bad day too but manages to ask you about yours in a caring and pleasant manner. Could you respond in a warm, caring and pleasant manner? When you are having the worst day, can you say 'can I have a few minutes/hours/days to respond to that?' rather than have a horrible reaction? What does it take to fix your attitude?

____

____

____

____

WEEK TWENTY-SEVEN PROJECT

Ask the following people the following questions and record their responses.

Mom/Dad/Guardian

Best Friend

Favorite teacher

Grandmother /Aunt/Favorite family member

Church leader/mentor

1. How do see/perceive me? What caused that perception? Is there anything that I can do to improve that perception?

____

____

____

____

____

2. What do you see for my future? How do you visualize that? Can you help me to see and prepare for it?

____

____

____

____

---

3. Name 3 great things about me. Name 3 areas where I need to improve.

____

____

____

____

4. How can I make our relationship better?

____

____

____

____

5. Do you have any advice for me?

____

____

____

____

WEEK TWENTY-SEVEN JOURNAL

WEEK TWENTY-EIGHT

Weapons for Warfare

The Armor of God

[10] Finally, be strong in the Lord and in his mighty power. [11] Put on the full armor of God, so that you can take your stand against the devil's schemes. [12] For our struggle is not against flesh and blood, but against the rulers, against the authorities, against the powers of this dark world and against the spiritual forces of evil in the heavenly realms. [13] Therefore put on the full armor of God, so that when the day of evil comes, you may be able to stand your ground, and after you have done everything, to stand. [14] Stand firm then, with the belt of truth buckled around your waist, with the breastplate of righteousness in place, [15] and with your feet fitted with the readiness that comes from the gospel of peace. [16] In addition to all this, take up the shield of faith, with which you can extinguish all the flaming arrows of the evil one. [17] Take the helmet of salvation and the sword of the Spirit, which is the word of God. [18] And pray in the Spirit on all occasions with all kinds of prayers and requests. With this in mind, be alert and always keep on praying for all the Lord's people.

Ephesians 6:10-18

Armor is designed to protect you from your enemy. Fighting happens. The enemy is persistent. The armor is not optional. It is provided for your protection (verse 11).

The clarification about warfare is that warfare is not against flesh and blood. Warfare is against rulers, against the authorities, against the powers of this dark world and against the spiritual forces of evil in the heavenly realms (verse 12). This is the devil and all of its details. The devil uses individuals to carry out his schemes but the people are not who you are fighting. It may seem like it but it is really the devil using that person. Often you will not realize that you are being used by the devil.

It is hard to be effective without the proper equipment. You are hard to protect without the equipment provided for you. Wear it. Know it. Study it. Own it. Share it.

The belt of truth buckled around your waist—tell the truth, support the truth, seek the truth, and honor the truth (verse 14).

The breastplate of righteousness—get near to righteousness, be righteous, do the right thing and seek righteousness (verse 14).

Feet fitted with the gospel of peace—be prepared to be peaceful and to share and spread peace (verse 15).

The shield of faith believing the God that we are serving is God and able to do exceedingly, abundantly, above all that we ask or think. This shield is fueled by faith so that the arrows which come to you will be extinguished because of God's power through your faith (verse 16).

The helmet of salvation is the saving grace of God which you wear on your head for protection (verse 17). The sword of the spirit is the word of God—the Bible, which you will need to read, study, meditate, and study. And use for understanding the directions and the paths where you trod (verse 17).

Paul is known for prayer so in verse 18, he encourages prayer for one another and prayer for yourself. What do you pray for? Everything. Absolutely everything. Grades. Friends. Teachers. School safety. Parents. Fear. Love. Trust. Sports. Loyalty. Wisdom. Knowledge. Retention. Recall. Attentiveness. Everything.

Now understand the armor does not have a back. You will not have your back to the enemy, so you need only the front. God is covering you completely. You will be attacked by the enemy. You will have fights. Winning versus losing is based on God's will but in order to do His will, you have to adorn the gear—the Armor.

Armor is impressive. It stops hurt and harm and danger. Hurt intended to keep you away from God, His will and His healing. Hurt that would distance you from a loving God.

Harm which causes irreparable damage. Damage which costs years to repair, maybe even decades.

Danger that is designed to kill, steal and destroy. Danger which destroys the details of your life and you are next.

The armor protects you from all of that, because God designed it and God created it and God provides it.

How do I put on all of this armor? First, realizing there is only one physical unit, the Bible. All other pieces are based on your spiritual relationship with God, Jesus and the Holy Spirit.

Tell the truth. Live the truth. Be truth. Truth. This is difficult. The truth hurts. The truth distances fake and lies. Don't be part of that distance. The world will tell you not to tell the truth, however the Bible affirms that the truth shall set you free.

Telling the truth and living in truth may be challenging initially but stick with the truth. It is easier to manage. It is hard to forget. Telling the truth is hard to receive sometimes but a whole lot more healthy. Seek the truth. Be the truth.

Righteousness. Well, who is righteous? This is a hard topic to cover. Not many are righteous, but you have to strive to be righteous. At your age, you can define righteous for your age group and yourself. Doing the right thing is part of righteousness. Following the righteous way can be difficult sometimes.

This means no cheating at school, which includes copying the answers from the internet or a friend. This also means not sex until marriage. Further, no lying, stealing, gossiping, hating, betraying your friends, and other socially—accepted sins which divide people and cause drama is relationships. Stop being messy and causing havoc. Positive activities and attitudes and peace needs to be your behavior.

Peace. Hard to achieve. Understandably so. Maybe you don't know peace because you do not see peace at home or at school. Peace means when discord happens, seeking the best possible outcome is peaceful. Bringing feuding friends together is peaceful. Peace means finding a bright side to what seems bad. Peace is also being able to provide a reasonable solution to a horrible problem. For some, peace means quiet, stillness and rest. Whatever peace means to you and how it changes over time, be peaceful. Work for peace.

Faith will be difficult if you don't think you have any faith. Faith is belief based on no security of what you think should happen. Faith is believing in God for His unbelievable and miraculous. Faith is sharing God with others (Hebrews 11).

Salvation is your relationship with God and Jesus. Take care of your salvation. Nothing should come between you and the love of God. Let no one and NOTHING come between you and your Lord and Savior. Your salvation has the perfect power to bring others to Christ as well.

The sword—the Bible. Read. Read. Read. Learn. Meditate. Share. Study. Memorize. Internalize. Hide His word in your heart so that you don't sin against God (Psalm 119:11).

Then lastly, pray. Just talk to God. Pray for yourself and others. Pray.

These are your weapons. Reach for these weapons. Not those weapons which are detrimental to you and possibly to others: drugs, sex, skipping school, and other coping mechanisms.

Remember that the devil will use whoever shows up to be used, just make sure that it is not you who allows yourself to be used. Check your behavior, then decide to walk away from behavior that reflects the devil rather than God.

WEEK TWENTY-EIGHT REFLECTION

1. What did you consider a weapon before these scriptures? Who did you think we were fighting?

____

____

____

____

2. How will these scriptures help you to fight now? How do you share these concepts with others?

____

____

____

____

3. How will you change your "bad" behaviors (for example: messy, liar, etc.)?

____

____

____

____

4. Do you ever let the devil use you without your knowledge? With your knowledge? Explain.

____

____

____

____

5.   What area(s) do you need to improve upon? How will you do that?

____

____

____

____

WEEK TWENTY-EIGHT PROJECT

List your favorite scriptures of these nine verses. Describe why.

____

____

____

____

____

____

____

____

____

____

____

____

____

____

____

____

WEEK TWENTY-EIGHT JOURNAL

WEEK TWENTY-NINE

God Made You a Girl

Proverbs 31:10—31

God made you a girl! What does that mean? Why does it matter? God made you a girl because He gave you some special attributes and characteristics. When He created females as a companion to man, He had some special ideas in mind. First, He created us as the 'weaker vessel.' (1 Peter 3:7) This is the expectation of strength, where God designed us to depend on Him and the men assigned to us. This is not popular with feminist who do not want to appear weaker or actually be weaker than a man. Being the weaker vessel means that God provides protection. This protection includes keeping our hearts and minds safe, which in these times is critical.

Secondly, He created you in His image. He created you loving, righteous, caring and special. Those are characteristics which are hard to maintain if you get too close to the world. We are to work hard to maintain that image. Image is not for image sake but for the relationship with God. Unfortunately, God is in competition for His very own creations. Daily.

Thirdly, girls are the pathway to life. Everyone is born to a mother—a girl. God chose us to birth His creations. We should also take this role seriously.

Fourthly, we are communicators. God trusts us to share information with Him and others. God should be able to communicate with you, such that if God gives you a message to give to someone else He can trust that it will be delivered the way He conveyed it. If not, you will disappoint God. God depends on us to communicate with Him about the concerns we have, any praise reports, any prayers.

Fifth, God defined you as a nurturer—that is how you are built. You understand some things differently and possibly better than boys.

Sixth, God is listening to you. He is prepared to supply all of your needs according to His will. God made you a girl.

Seventh, God made you a girl on purpose. Jeremiah 1:5 states, "Before I formed you in your mother's womb, I knew you." God did not need an ultra sound to know your gender—He created you a girl! He does not need the radiologist to confirm what God decided thousands of years ago.

When God made you a girl, He gave you a job. These scriptures outline some of God's expectations and while they seem only for grown-ups, the principles can be applied to our daily life. The woman in these scriptures exercises good judgement, wise choices, healthy relationships, and serious work ethic.

He also made you to serve Him in your endeavors—in all that you do. What is God's will for your life? What does He want you to do?

Whatever it is, it is important to understand that you should be prepared to do it well. All of the time.

This woman is a classy lady. She is an entrepreneur. She is a leader. She works hard. She is respected. She is watched for how to be a woman. She is an example in the community.

She is an example for all women. She makes life seem amazing. She makes all women wonder how she does it. The answer to that is the guidance and the will of God.

How can we do that? 'That seems like so much to do and what if I fail?'

Well, that is a tall order and offers much to strive for and that is certainly understandable. However, with God nothing is impossible.

What are you going to do as a girl? First, achieve all that you desire. Because you are a girl—for no other reason than you are a girl. Being a girl wasn't always this glamourous. Being a woman was formerly a disgrace. Women were not equal to men. In some cultures, women are not allowed to show their faces or their hair. They could not own property. Clearly, that is not what God intended since He wrote this scripture before that time, even today.

Your girliness had nothing to do with you but a choice that God made for you. He has a plan for you that is amazing. It will overwhelm even you. The plan does require your participation, but not your consent. Not even you can sabotage God's plan for you. You can attempt to delay His plan, but derail and sabotage, you will not.

You are a girl. The definition may have some slight variations but the total is that you are special because God said so. He made you so He defines you—He defines you as special. He loves you unconditionally and He is the only one who does.

God made you a girl.

WEEK TWENTY-NINE REFLECTION

1.   What is your definition of yourself as a girl? How closely aligned is that to God's definition?

____

____

____

2.   Which scriptures will you apply to your life within 30 days?

____

____

____

3.   90 days?

____

____

____

4.   6 months?

____

____

____

____

5. One year?

____

____

____

____

6. Five years?

____

____

____

____

7. Ten years?

____

____

____

____

WEEK TWENTY-NINE PROJECT

1.   Create a poster of your best photos of yourself.

2.   Add words which make you smile, feel powerful and be inspired.

3.   Add your favorite scripture.

4.   Place the poster where you can see daily without any extra work (not behind a door, etc.).

WEEK TWENTY-NINE JOURNAL

WEEK THIRTY

Today Affects Tomorrow
Proverbs 31:10—31

The great thing about life is that everyone starts at the same place—birth and everyone has the same requirements—school. For the most parts, everyone had the same consequences as well. Consider the storms of 6 women/girls.

Woman #1.

She graduated sixth in her graduating class. She was accepted into three universities of her choice with huge scholarships at each one. She finished one year before she decided to leave school and get married to her high school boyfriend, who was across the nation working. She eventually had two children with two different men.

She never completed college and now is having a hard time finding a job earning more than $12/hour, which at full-time hours before taxes and benefit deductions totals $24860. If you multiply that by 85%, then you have an estimate of her take home pay. Then divide that by 24, the number of paychecks she would receive if she is paid twice monthly. That is less than $1000 per pay period. What does that money buy? What do you think that she thinks about her current life? Do you think that she regrets her decision to leave college? Especially since the marriage ended as well. What should she do now?

Woman #2.

She was caught smoking drugs after accepting a college scholarship to a division one school. She runs track. Great academic grades. She was caught through random drug testing. She was dismissed from the team, charged with possession, and then tragedy really struck: she could no longer afford school.

She found out the hard way that she could no longer get financial aid because of the drug charges, so she could not even borrow the money to go to school.

Her dreams of becoming an attorney just vanished. Why did she try drugs? Did she resolve her issue by using marijuana? Did she cause more problems than the one she originally had? How can she solve her problem? What will she do now? Based on what you know, what will you do differently?

Woman #3.

She had sex with her prom date. She did not want to but he persuaded her that it would be fun. She had heard from her friends that if she didn't have sex with him, then he would have sex with someone else. She didn't want to lose him to someone else, so against her better judgement, they had sex.

As she prepares for college camp, she finds out that she is pregnant. She decides to abort the baby. She never tells anyone, but she regrets if often. She never sees sex the same again. She never treats men the same again.

When she gets married, she is told that the scar tissue from the abortion has interfered with her ability to have children. She is devastated. Her marriage may not survive.

Woman #4

She was drinking and drank so much that she does not know if she hit someone or not. She left a party but no one thought to tell her no! While she never knew conclusively, she always wondered how her drinking caused pain.

Woman #5

She had sex just for the sake of sex, or maybe it was to cope with all that she had endured: rape, molestation, low self-esteem from lack of acceptance, and not being able to have children because of the damage from the rape.

Woman #6

She tried 'handlebars' while in 7th grade. A guy from her apartment complex gave the drugs to her. She was high for three hours before her math teacher found out. Her mother was finally called to pick her up. The math teacher talked to her before she left asking several questions: 1) Did she know him? 2) How long had he been watching her? 3) Could he see her weak self-esteem? 4) What was the next time going to cost her: money, sex, or selling the drugs to pay for her own? 5) Did you have sex with him? 6) What is going to happen if he demands sex in exchange?

Today and Tomorrow

Between drugs, sex, alcohol, cutting, and other addictive behaviors, you have to consider the consequences to those activities.

Drugs have addictive effects, possible school suspension, removal from sports, and other adverse body effects. Can you afford any of that to happen? Why drugs? Is that the best way to cope and/or experiment?

Sex is another big issue. Sex involves sharing your soul with the other person, as well as your body. Sex is a spiritual experience, so this should be used sparingly because the consequences are too severe. Further, this soul sharing needs to be consented to mutually. It never goes well when the two people feel differently and respond differently after the act.

Consider the effects of sex: you are blissful and 'in-love' with him after your first encounter, your very first time. Whew! You are thinking about him all of the time. He made you feel special. You are special but not because of the sex. So you are devastated when you arrive at the locker that you share with him to find him kissing someone else.

In your heart and mind, you are thinking we just had sex! But clearly is does not mean the same to him. What will you do? How will you respond? How will you recover from that heart break? How did you feel? Remember that this was a scenario, but someone experiences that situation daily. No, it does not get easier as you get older. It still happens in adulthood. It is risky to give your soul away through your body. Try to not to share your body with a mate that is not committed to you, more than you are committed to him.

Alcoholism is on the rise amongst your age group. One thing that you do not know is whether or not you are predisposed to alcohol addiction. Predisposed means that you will be more likely to be addicted to alcohol because of an hereditary background. You may need to know that before you start drinking and using drugs as well.

Suicide, suicide attempts, and activities based on suicidal desires are at an all-time high. This includes cutting. Those escapes are life-threatening and quite detrimental to your life. Cutting may leave permanent marks—permanent reminders of the mental state and emotional conditions and social situations that you have going on.

Cutting is an escape which could lead to death. You could actually bleed out by cutting because you could cut the vein which you cannot stop bleeding alone or before someone can find you to stop the bleeding. Please seek the help of an adult if you feel the need to cut. Or any suicidal thoughts or activities. Find the nearest adult that you trust with whom you can talk, so that you can get the help you need.

God created you to be a great asset to Him. But you need to be functional to do so. You want to craft your testimony carefully so that you can share it all with others. Sometimes when people are ashamed of their past/testimony, they are reluctant to share that testimony. Your testimony is designed to help others to grow, to learn what to do, and what not to do.

All of these activities are a reflection of a low-esteem desperately in need of repair. Work daily to recover from that which ails you. Young lady, please avoid these behaviors if at all possible.

God created you to be a girl that will honor His words and His name and to bring Him glory. He has prepared some assignments for you and He is waiting for you to answer Him and obey. He is waiting.

WEEK THIRTY REFLECTION

1. Share your thoughts about woman 1. What would you do differently? What would you do instead?

____

____

____

____

2. Share your thoughts about woman 2. What would you do differently? What would you do instead?

____

____

____

3. Share your thoughts about woman 3. What would you do differently? What would you do instead?

____

____

____

4. Share your thoughts about woman 4. What would you do differently? What would you do instead?

____

____

____

____

5.   Share your thoughts about woman 5. What would you do differently? What would you do instead?

____

____

____

____

6.   Share your thoughts about woman 6. What would you do differently? What would you do instead?

____

____

____

____

7.   What will you do when presented with the concept of sex? Will you say yes? If you already said yes, did you regret it?

____

____

____

____

8.   How will you recover from a failed relationship where sex was involved?

9. Why try drugs? How can you become strong enough to say no? What happens when you become addicted? What if you die from the use of the drug?

10. What if you are unable to play sports or do other activities because you failed a drug test? Do you know that careers do random drug tests on their employees? The results could be your loss of employment. Can you afford to lose your job due to drug usage?

11. Do you know that drug charges (because of possession) will prevent you from receiving financial aid? How will you pay for school?

12. What happens if the drugs cause your organs to shut down? Research the effects of drug use.

13. Have you ever considered suicide? Why? Have you told your parent(s)? How would you commit suicide if you attempted?

14. Do you cut yourself? Do you know what cutting is? Do you know that those scars can be permanent?

15. What can we do to help you feel better about yourself?

---

16. How would your parents and friends feel if you killed yourself?

WEEK THIRTY PROJECT

1. Research funeral costs. Plan your funeral. Ask your parents if you have insurance.

2. Research the effects of drugs on your body and your life.

3. Research the suicide data for teenage girls.

4. Research the teen pregnancy rates. Adoption rates. Abortion rates.

5. Write a letter to your family and friends about your feelings.

WEEK THIRTY JOURNAL

REFLECTIONS

REFLECTIONS

REFLECTIONS

REFLECTIONS

APPENDIX

Your Testimony

Your testimony is your experience with God and the results of that experience. This includes your first encounter with Christ to your current life.

Consider the answers to the following questions to develop your testimony:

1. When did you first meet Christ?
2. How do you share how you met Christ with others?
3. What have your encounters with God been like?
4. What is your relationship with God like?
5. What danger has He kept you from?
6. What have you done that would have sabotaged God's work if He had not stopped you?
7. What has happened that you realized that only God was in charge to make this happen?

The Names of God

(1) *Elohim*: The plural form of *EL*, meaning "strong one." It is used of false gods, but when used of the true God, it is a plural of majesty and intimates the trinity. It is especially used of God's sovereignty, creative work, mighty work for Israel and in relation to His sovereignty (Isa. 54:5; Jer. 32:27; Gen. 1:1; Isa. 45:18; Deut. 5:23; 8:15; Ps. 68:7).

Compounds of *El*:

- ***El Shaddai:*** "God Almighty." The derivation is uncertain. Some think it stresses God's loving supply and comfort; others His power as the Almighty one standing on a mountain and who corrects and chastens (Gen. 17:1; 28:3; 35:11; Ex. 6:1; Ps. 91:1, 2).
- ***El Elyon:*** "The Most High God." Stresses God's strength, sovereignty, and supremacy (Gen. 14:19; Ps. 9:2; Dan. 7:18, 22, 25).
- ***El Olam*:** "The Everlasting God." Emphasizes God's unchangeableness and is connected with His inexhaustibleness (Gen. 16:13).

(2) *Yahweh (YHWH):* Comes from a verb which means "to exist, be." This, plus its usage, shows that this name stresses God as the independent and self-existent God of revelation and redemption (Gen. 4:3; Ex. 6:3 (cf. 3:14); 3:12).

Compounds of *Yahweh:* Strictly speaking, these compounds are designations or titles which reveal additional facts about God's character.

- ***Yahweh Jireh (Yireh):*** "The Lord will provide." Stresses God's provision for His people (Gen. 22:14).
- ***Yahweh Nissi:*** "The Lord is my Banner." Stresses that God is our rallying point and our means of victory; the one who fights for His people (Ex. 17:15).
- ***Yahweh Shalom:*** "The Lord is Peace." Points to the Lord as the means of our peace and rest (Jud. 6:24).
- ***Yahweh Sabbaoth:*** "The Lord of Hosts." A military figure portraying the Lord as the commander of the armies of heaven (1 Sam. 1:3; 17:45).
- ***Yahweh Maccaddeshcem*:** "The Lord your Sanctifier." Portrays the Lord as our means of sanctification or as the one who sets believers apart for His purposes (Ex. 31:13).
- ***Yahweh Ro'i:*** "The Lord my Shepherd." Portrays the Lord as the Shepherd who cares for His people as a shepherd cares for the sheep of his pasture (Ps. 23:1).
- ***Yahweh Tsidkenu:*** "The Lord our Righteousness." Portrays the Lord as the means of our righteousness (Jer. 23:6).

- ***Yahweh Shammah***: "The Lord is there." Portrays the Lord's personal presence in the millennial kingdom (Ezek. 48:35).
- ***Yahweh Elohim Israel:*** "The Lord, the God of Israel." Identifies Yahweh as the God of Israel in contrast to the false gods of the nations (Jud. 5:3.; Isa. 17:6).

(3) ***Adonai:*** Like *Elohim*, this too is a plural of majesty. The singular form means "master, owner." Stresses man's relationship to God as his master, authority, and provider (Gen. 18:2; 40:1; 1 Sam. 1:15; Ex. 21:1-6; Josh. 5:14).

(4) ***Theos***: Greek word translated "God." Primary name for God used in the New Testament. Its use teaches: (1) *He is the only true God* (Matt. 23:9; Rom. 3:30); (2) *He is unique* (1 Tim. 1:17; John 17:3; Rev. 15:4; 16:7); (3) *He is transcendent* (Acts 17:24; Heb. 3:4; Rev. 10:6); (4) *He is the Savior* (John 3:16; 1 Tim. 1:1; 2:3; 4:10). This name is used of Christ as God in John 1:1, 18; 20:28; 1 John 5:20; Tit. 2:13; Rom. 9:5; Heb. 1:8; 2 Pet. 1:1.

(5) ***Kurios***: Greek word translated "Lord." Stresses authority and supremacy. While it can mean sir (John 4:11), owner (Luke 19:33), master (Col. 3:22), or even refer to idols (1 Cor. 8:5) or husbands (1 Pet. 3:6), it is used mostly as the equivalent of *Yahweh* of the Old Testament. It too is used of Jesus Christ meaning (1) Rabbi or Sir (Matt. 8:6); (2) God or Deity (John 20:28; Acts 2:36; Rom. 10:9; Phil. 2:11).

(6) ***Despotes***: Greek word translated "Master." Carries the idea of ownership while *kurios* stressed supreme authority (Luke 2:29; Acts 4:24; Rev. 6:10; 2 Pet. 2:1; Jude 4).

(7) ***Father***: A distinctive New Testament revelation is that through faith in Christ, God becomes our personal Father. Father is used of God in the Old Testament only 15 times while it is used of God 245 times in the New Testament. As a name of God, it stresses God's loving care, provision, discipline, and the way we are to address God in prayer (Matt. 7:11; Jam. 1:17; Heb. 12:5-11; John 15:16; 16:23; Eph. 2:18; 3:15; 1 Thess. 3:11).

Source: http://www.agapebiblestudy.com/documents/the%20many%20names%20of%20god.htm

Prayer

A Short How To Guide

The prayers which are most effective follow the following "rules:"

- ➢ It is a conversation with God.
- ➢ Be honest with God.
- ➢ This is a relationship.
- ➢ God is to be praised, worshiped and glorified.
- ➢ God likes His word prayed back to Him.
- ➢ This is not a list of stuff you want.
- ➢ Think of more than yourself when you pray.
- ➢ Be authentic with God and yourself.
- ➢ Be prepared for people to ask you about your prayer life and faith.
- ➢ Do not worry about big words or long sentences.
- ➢ Please know that God is not taking revenge on others for you, and vice versa.
- ➢ Please prayer in the name of Jesus.
- ➢ There is no correct way to pray.

Scriptures on Prayer

Matthew 6:9-14

1 Thessalonians 5:17

Matthew 26:

John 17

Prayer Requests

Prayer Journal

1. What are you asking God for?

2. What are you hoping God will do?

3. What are you expecting from God?

4. What has God already done to exceed your expectations?

5. What has God done to get your attention?

6. What has He shown about Himself and you?

____

____

____

____

____

____

____

____

____

Favorite Scriptures

Numbers 6:24-26

[24] The LORD bless you and keep you;

[25] the LORD make his face shine on you and be gracious to you;

[26] the LORD turn his face toward you and give you peace."

Jeremiah 1:5

[5] "Before I formed you in the womb I knew[a] you, before you were born I set you apart; I appointed you as a prophet to the nations."

Jeremiah 29:11

[11] For I know the plans I have for you," declares the LORD, "plans to prosper you and not to harm you, plans to give you hope and a future.

Psalm 8:1

[1] LORD, our Lord, how excellent is Your name in all the earth!

Psalm 19:14

[14] May these words of my mouth and this meditation of my heart be pleasing in your sight, LORD, my Rock and my Redeemer.

30 WEEK BIBLE STUDY FOR TEEN GIRLS

Psalm 46:1, 10

[1] God is our refuge and strength, an ever-present help in trouble. [10] "Be still, and know that I am God."

Psalm 119:11

[11] I have hidden your word in my heart that I might not sin against you.

Psalm 139:14

[14] I praise you because I am fearfully and wonderfully made; your works are wonderful, I know that full well.

Proverbs 3:5-6

[5] Trust in the LORD with all your heart and lean not on your own understanding;
[6] in all your ways acknowledge him, and he will make your paths straight.

Proverbs 23:7 (KJV)

[7] For as he thinketh in his heart, so is he: Eat and drink, saith he to thee; but his heart is not with thee.

Habakkuk 2:2

[2] Then the LORD replied: "Write down the revelation and make it plain on tablets so that a herald[a] may run with it.

Matthew 11:28, 30

[28] "Come to me, all you who are weary and heavy-ladened, and I will give you rest.

[30] For my yoke is easy and my burden is light."

Matthew 14:31

[31] Immediately Jesus reached out his hand and caught him. "You of little faith," he said, "why did you doubt?"

Matthew 22:37

[37] Jesus replied: "'Love the Lord your God with all your heart and with all your soul and with all your mind.

Matthew 28:19-20

[19] Therefore go and make disciples of all nations, baptizing them in[a] the name of the Father and of the Son and of the Holy Spirit, [20] and teaching them to obey everything I have commanded you. And surely I am with you always, to the very end of the age."

Luke 9:24

[23] Then he said to them all: "If anyone would come after me, he must deny himself and take up his cross daily and follow me. [24] For whoever wants to save his life will lose it, but whoever loses his life for me will save it.

Luke 23:34

[34] Jesus said, "Father, forgive them, for they do not know what they are doing."[a] And they divided up his clothes by casting lots.

John 1:1-2

[1] In the beginning was the Word, and the Word was with God, and the Word was God. [2] He was with God in the beginning.

John 3:16

[16] "For God so loved the world that he gave his one and only Son,[a] that whoever believes in him shall not perish but have eternal life.

John 3:30

[30] He must become greater; I must become less.

John 11:35

[35] Jesus wept.

Romans 8:26

[26] In the same way, the Spirit helps us in our weakness. We do not know what we ought to pray for, but the Spirit himself intercedes for us with groans that words cannot express.

1 Corinthians 10:13

[13] No temptation has seized you except what is common to man. And God is faithful; he will not let you be tempted beyond what you can bear. But when you are tempted, he will also provide a way out so that you can stand up under it.

Galatians 5:22-23

[22] But the fruit of the Spirit is love, joy, peace, patience, kindness, goodness, faithfulness, [23] gentleness and self-control. Against such things there is no law.

Ephesians 3:14-21

[14] For this reason I kneel before the Father, [15] from whom his whole family[a] in heaven and on earth derives its name. [16] I pray that out of his glorious riches he may strengthen you with power through his Spirit in your inner being, [17] so that Christ may dwell in your hearts through faith. And I pray that you, being rooted and established in love, [18] may have power, together with all the saints, to grasp how wide and long and high and deep is the love of Christ, [19] and to know this love that surpasses knowledge—that you may be filled to the measure of all the fullness of God. [20] Now unto him who is able to do immeasurably more than all we ask or imagine, according to his power that is at work within us, [21] to him be glory in the church and in Christ Jesus throughout all generations, for ever and ever! Amen.

Ephesians 4:26-27

[26] "In your anger do not sin"[a]: Do not let the sun go down while you are still angry, [27] and do not give the devil a foothold.

Ephesians 4:32

[32] Be kind and compassionate to one another, forgiving each other, just as in Christ God forgave you.

Philippians 4:7

[7] And the peace of God, which transcends all understanding, will guard your hearts and your minds in Christ Jesus.

Philippians 4:13-17

[13] I can do everything through him who gives me strength. [14] Yet it was good of you to share in my troubles. [15] Moreover, as you Philippians know, in the early days of your acquaintance with the gospel, when I set out from Macedonia, not one church shared with me in the matter of giving and receiving, except you only; [16] for even when I

was in Thessalonica, you sent me aid again and again when I was in need. [17] Not that I am looking for a gift, but I am looking for what may be credited to your account.

Colossians 3:23

[23] Whatever you do, work at it with all your heart, as working for the Lord, not for men,

1 Thessalonians 5:17

[17] pray continually;

Hebrews 11:6

[6] And without faith it is impossible to please God, because anyone who comes to him must believe that he exists and that he rewards those who earnestly seek him.

Hebrews 13:5b

[5] Keep your lives free from the love of money and be content with what you have, because God has said, "Never will I leave you; never will I forsake you."

James 1:2-5

[2] Consider it pure joy, my brothers, whenever you face trials of many kinds, [3] because you know that the testing of your faith develops perseverance. [4] Perseverance must finish its work so that you may be mature and complete, not lacking anything. [5] If any of you lacks wisdom, he should ask God, who gives generously to all without finding fault, and it will be given to him.

Jude 24

[24]Now unto him that is able to keep you from falling, and to present you faultless before the presence of his glory with exceeding joy,

Revelation 3:16

[16] So, because you are lukewarm—neither hot nor cold—I am about to spit you out of my mouth.

Goals

goal [gohl] *noun*

the result or achievement toward <u>which</u> effort is directed; aim; end.

The questions that you answer when developing goals are as follows:

1. What do I want to accomplish for God, with God, because of God?
2. When do I want to accomplish this by? What does God's timing look like?
3. Who is going to help me and hold me accountable? Who has God sent my way for this matter?
4. What do you do when you do not meet the goals as planned? What will God do in the meantime?
5. Who do you share your successes with? How will God use my achievement to help others?

Goals

Goals	By When	Who

Mission Statement

A personal mission statement is based on habit 2 of <u>7 Habits of Highly Effective People</u> called begin with the end in mind. In one's life, the most effective way to begin with the end in mind is to develop a mission statement. One that focuses what you want to be in terms of character and what you want to do in reference to contribution of achievements. Writing a mission statement can be the most important activity an individual can take to truly lead one's life.

Victor Hugo once said there is nothing as powerful as an idea whose time has finally come, you may call it a credo, a philosophy, you may call it a purpose statement, it's not as important as to what you call it, no it's how you define your definition. That mission and vision statement is more powerful, more significant, more influential, than the baggage of the past, or even the accumulated noise of the present.

What is a mission statement you ask? Personal mission statements based on correct principles are like a personal constitution, the basis for making major, life-directing decisions, the basis for making daily decisions in the midst of the circumstances and emotions that affect our lives.

Your statement may be a few words or several pages, but it is not a "to do" list. It reflects your uniqueness and must speak to you powerfully about the person you are and the person you are becoming.

Why should you write a personal mission statement?

Numerous experts on leadership and personal development emphasize how vital it is for you to craft your own personal vision for your life. Warren Bennis, Stephen Covey, Peter Senge, and others point out that a powerful vision can help you succeed far beyond where you'd be without one. That vision can propel you and inspire those around you to reach their own dreams.

Q: How do I go about creating my Personal Mission Statement?

A: A Mission Statement is defined as having goals and a deadline. This is opposed to the notion that a Mission Statement is just a bunch of flowery, general phrases like, "I will be the best business person I can be."

What should you include when writing a great personal mission statement?

- describe your best characteristics and how you express them
- have specific, measurable outcomes (or goals)
- have a deadline — for example, December 31st 2012, or a year from today.

When Stephen Covey talks about 'mission statement' in this quote, he is referring to the articulation of your life purpose. "If you don't set your goals based upon your Mission Statement, you may be climbing the ladder of success only to realize, when you get to the top, you're on the WRONG BUILDING." **Stephen Covey – 7 Habits of Highly Effective People.**

Mission Statement Example – Poor (It's more like a Vision Statement)

"I aspire to start my own business. I want to help others and be a better businesswoman. I will deliver the best food with the highest service levels." Jane

Mission Statement Example – Better

"I will start my business within 3 months and plan to grow it to $500,000 in revenues within a year. Using this success, my staff and I will spread the word to local schools and businesses about eco-friendly food production in order that we reach at least 100 people within the same time frame. My purpose will be to massively add value to our local community in measurable ways that have a real impact on people's health now and in the future," Jane.

What to do with your Mission Statement?

So now we have a mission, we can set a range of goals on the road to achieving your outcomes and dreams. Your values are clarified and should be in line with the goals you want to achieve in life so you should find it easier to make decisions and to do the "right thing" because you can simply ask yourself, "Will this help me achieve my mission?"

You can even put your mission statement in an area where your family or even co-workers will see it. For, a mission statement defines who you are and what you stand for. This lets people see how you think and feel, which in turn, will help them respect, think and act in line with your values too.

Mission Statement

Vision Statement

A personal vision/mission statement is the framework for creating a powerful life.

Your personal vision statement provides the direction necessary to guide the course of your days and the choices you make about your life.

The idea is to craft a broad based idea about your life and what will really make it exciting and fulfilling, that's your life vision. From the vision, you craft a more focused and action orientated "mission" statement based on "purpose." And finally you get to a list of goals, wishes, desires and needs.

In his book 'The Success Principles,' Jack Canfield tells us that in order to create a balanced and successful life; your vision needs to include the following seven areas:

1. work and career
2. finances
3. recreation and free time
4. health and fitness
5. relationships
6. personal goals
7. contribution to the larger community

It does not include the distinctive ways that you intend to accomplish your purpose.

Why Write a Personal Vision Statement?

To express:

- your purpose
- your life's dream
- your core values & beliefs
- what you want for yourself
- what you want to contribute to others
- what you want to be

Characteristics of a Vision Statement:

- Engages your heart & spirit
- Taps into embedded concerns & needs
- Asserts what you want to create
- Is something worth going for
- Provides meaning to the work you do
- Is a little cloudy and grand
- Is simple
- Is a living document
- Provides a starting place from which to get more specificity
- Is based on quality and dedication

Key Elements of a Vision Statement:

- Written down and referred to daily
- Written in present tense, as if it has already been completed
- Includes a variety of activities and time frames
- Filled with descriptive details that anchor it to reality

What Visions Are Not:

- A mission statement: "Why do we exist now?"
- A strategic plan: "How do we plan to get there?"
- A set of objectives: "We will accomplish X by Y time to Z% target audience."

Use these questions to guide your thoughts:

- What are the ten things you most enjoy doing? Be honest. These are the ten things without which your weeks, months, and years would feel incomplete.
- What three things must you do every single day to feel fulfilled in your work?
- What are your five-six most important values?
- Your life has a number of important facets or dimensions, all of which deserve some attention in your personal vision statement.
- Write one important goal for each of them: physical, spiritual, work or career, family, social relationships, financial security, mental improvement and attention, and fun.
- If you never had to work another day in your life, how would you spend your time instead of working?
- When your life is ending, what will you regret not doing, seeing, or achieving?
- What strengths have other people commented on about you and your accomplishments? What strengths do you see in yourself?

Vision Statement

Values Statement

A personal **value** is absolute or relative and ethical value, the assumption of which can be the basis for ethical action. A *value system* is a set of consistent values and measures. A *principle value* is a foundation upon which other values and measures of integrity are based.

Some values are physiologically determined and are normally considered objective, such as a desire to avoid physical pain or to seek pleasure. Other values are considered subjective, vary across individuals and cultures, and are in many ways aligned with belief and belief systems. Types of values include ethical/moral values, doctrinal/ideological (religious, political) values, social values, and aesthetic values. It is debated whether some values that are not clearly physiologically determined, such as altruism, are intrinsic, and whether some, such as acquisitiveness, should be classified as vices or virtues.

Values can be defined as broad preference concerning appropriate courses of action or outcomes. As such, values reflect a person's sense of right and wrong or what "ought" to be. "Equal rights for all", "Excellence deserves admiration", and "People should be treated with respect and dignity" are representative of values. Values tend to influence attitudes and behavior.

Values Statement

Dreams List

Resources

www.onediagage.com

War Room (movie)

Akeelah and the Bee (movie)

Coach Carter (movie)

The Hive (movie)

<u>As We Grow Together Daily Devotional for Expectant Couples</u>

<u>As We Grow Together Prayer Journal for Expectant Couples</u>

<u>The Blue Print: Poetry for the Soul</u>

<u>From Two to One: The Notebook for Couples</u>

<u>In Purple Ink: Poetry for the Spirit</u>

<u>Living a Whole Life: Sermons which Prompt, Provoke and Promote Life</u>

<u>Love Letters to God from a Teenage Girl</u>

<u>The Measure of a Woman: The Details of Her Soul</u>

<u>The Notebook: For Me, About Me, By Me</u>

<u>The Notebook for the Christian Teen</u>

<u>On This Journey Daily Devotional for Young People</u>

<u>On This Journey Prayer Journal for Young People</u>

30 WEEK BIBLE STUDY FOR TEEN GIRLS

<u>One Day More Than We Deserve Daily Devotional for the Growing Christian</u>

<u>One Day More Than We Deserve Prayer Journal for the Growing Christian</u>

<u>Promises, Promises: A Christian Novel</u>

<u>Tools for These Times: Timely Sermons for Uncertain Times</u>

<u>With An Anointed Voice: The Power of Prayer</u>

<u>Yielded and Submitted: A Woman's Journey for a Life Dedicated to God</u>

<u>Yielded and Submitted: A Woman's Journey for a Life Dedicated to God Prayers and Journal</u>

<u>Yielded and Submitted: A Woman's Journey for a Life Dedicated to God An Intimate Study</u>

<u>The Power of a Praying Woman</u> Stormie Omartian

<u>The Power of a Praying Wife</u> Stormie Omartian

<u>Discerning the Voice of God</u> Priscilla Shirer

<u>Kingdom Woman</u> Tony Evans and Crystal Evans Hurst

ACKNOWLEDGEMENTS

God, thank You for Your plans for me. Thank You for ***Queen in the Making 30 Week Bible Study for Teen Girls*** and choosing me to complete Your project. I just want to please You. Thank You for continuing to anoint me and to invest in me and my gifts, which keep surprising me. Thank You for loving and forgiving me.

Hillary and Nehemiah, thank you for supporting me and my endeavors. Thank you for loving me, especially when I do nothing without a pen and a clipboard, thank you for enduring my late nights, your ideas, the sounding board, the love and the support. Thank you for celebrating our legacy.

Kimberly 'Ann' Joiner, thank you for reading my work and offering your honest feedback. May your life be blessed for doing God's will.

To the girls who have raised their hands in need of this study. I don't know all of you, but the ones I do know, I apologies. I got it to you as quickly as I could. I love you!

To my prayer partners and to my accountability partners, thank you for the long talks and the powerful prayers and the encouragement. To my pastor and church family, thank you so much for your love and support.

Minister Onedia N. Gage seeks to share her outlandish pursuit of God with her prayers, study and meditation. She desires to share her faith in a manner which helps you do the same through her calling. She hopes that these words bless you.

Please feel free to contact and share your testimony. onediagage@onediagage.com, or @onediangage (twitter). www.onediagage.com

Blogtalkradio.com/onediagage

Youtube.com/onediagage

Facebook.com/onedia-gage-ministries

PREACHER ♦ ADVOCATE ♦ TEACHER ♦ FACILITATOR

CONFERENCE SPEAKER ♦ WORKSHOP LEADER

To invite Rev. Gage to speak to the teens at your church, women's ministry,

The full congregation or any other ministry.

Please contact us at: www.onedigage.com

@onediangage (twitter) ♦ onediagage@onediagage.com ♦ facebook.com/onediagageministries

youtube.com/onediagage ♦ blogtalkradio.com/onediagage ♦ ongage (Instagram)

Publishing

Do you have a book you want to write, but do not know what to do?

Do you have a book you need to publish but do not know how to start?

Would publishing move your career forward?

Let us help

onediagage@purpleink.net ♦ www.purpleink.net

281.740.5143 ♦ 512.715.4243